P9-CBR-813

Familiar Ground

Elizabeth Cox

Familiar Ground

Atheneum   New York   1984

For Nancy,
with all my good
wishes —

Elizabeth Cox
Dec. 9, 1986

*With gratitude to Yaddo and to the MacDowell Colony
for time and space in which to work.*

Excerpt from THE UNBEARABLE LIGHTNESS OF BEING *by Milan
Kundera, translated by Michael Henry Heim, English translation
copyright © 1984 by Harper & Row, Publishers, Inc., copyright ©
1984 by Milan Kundera, used by permission of Harper & Row
Publishers, Inc.*

Library of Congress Cataloging in Publication Data

Cox, Elizabeth.
    Familiar ground.

    I. Title.
PS3553.09183F3   1984ʻ 813ʹ.54   84–45055
ISBN 0–689–11474–5

Copyright © 1984 by Elizabeth Cox
All rights reserved
Published simultaneously in Canada by McClelland and Stewart Ltd.
Composition by Heritage Printers, Inc., Charlotte, North Carolina
Manufactured by Fairfield Graphics, Fairfield, Pennsylvania
Designed by Harry Ford
First Edition

For Jim,
Mike, and Beth

The idea of eternal return is a mysterious one: to think that everything recurs as we once experienced it, and that the recurrence itself recurs ad infinitum! . . . *In the world of eternal return the weight of unbearable responsibility lies heavy on every move we make. That is why Nietzsche called the idea of eternal return the heaviest of burdens (das schwerste Gewicht).*
. . . *The heavier the burden, the closer our lives come to the earth, the more real and truthful they become.*

The Unbearable Lightness of Being
Milan Kundera

Contents

Familiar Ground

 *A Public Place*

Jacob came to Sweetwater, Tennessee, by train. It was autumn and he felt unhoused in spirit, but he always felt that way in autumn. What brought Jacob back to Sweetwater was a letter from a woman who must be close to a hundred years old and a newspaper clipping that (though he had not read it in years) Jacob found he still knew almost by heart.

The train was one of the few trains left now for traveling, most being turned into boutiques or restaurants. This train went its route from Virginia to Tennessee, stopping at towns along the way to let off coal or passengers. And it seemed to Jacob that they didn't ride long before the train rumbled and squealed to its first blistering halt.

Jacob brushed a shock of hair from his forehead and removed his coat, a sportcoat made of soft wool, too hot for this day, but his favorite. He read and reread the clipping, hoping to find something not noticed before. But a small boy distracted him. The boy was running, swinging himself by the arms of seats. He stopped at intervals, giving anyone who might wish the chance to speak to him. Jacob nodded and the boy sat beside him, assured of welcome.

"Ever catch a fish?" the boy asked.

"Yeah. Did you?"

"Caught two."

"You did?"

3

"Caught two this big." The boy reached with his arms as wide as he could.

"I've never seen a fish that big. Where did you catch a fish that big?"

"It was some whales."

"Whales? No."

"Yep. Two whales." The boy looked Jacob straight in the eye. "I caught 'em."

"That's the most amazing thing I've ever heard," said Jacob. "What's your name?"

"David Harley Roberts." The boy scratched his head. His hair was cropped short and stuck up the same length all over. "What's yours?"

"Jacob Bechner. Jake."

"You call me Harley."

A woman's voice broke from the next car and the boy slipped from his seat, making a motion with his hand that indicated he would be right back. He pushed the curtain that separated the two cars. "David," the voice called. "Come clean up this mess."

The boy poked his head back through the curtain and held it beneath his chin. He looked as if he were in the shower. "She calls me David." He waited for Jacob to nod. "But my name's Harley. You call me Harley." He vanished again. Jacob watched the movement of the curtain regulate itself to the movement of the train, and was dozing when the boy returned and sat beside him.

"My Mama's asleep."

"So was I. She won't mind if you sit here?"

"Uh-uh." Harley stiffened his legs in front of him and Jacob thought he might say something about his shoes. "You know those whales I told you?"

"Yes."

"Do you believe that?"

4

"That's what you told me," said Jacob.

"I didn't catch them yet," said Harley. He lowered his legs. "But I could if I wanted to."

"Harley," said Jacob in a serious tone. "I look at it like this." And Harley looked at Jacob as if Jacob would tell him something profound and long-lasting. "You could if you wanted to."

The boy pulled a candy bar from his pocket. It was mashed and softened, but he offered it anyway. "Want some?" Jacob took it and halved it. They ate, licking the chocolate and using their fingers as spoons.

"Do you have kids?" Harley asked him.

"Yes. I have two sons. Well, one now. But he's not little anymore."

"I'm not little anymore either."

"No. I know." Jacob cleared his throat. "I mean, he's older now and has a family of his own."

"Do you know how old I am?"

"Nine." Jacob spoke this with conviction.

"Nope. I'm five." Harley swept the piece of paper clean with his finger and licked off the last of the chocolate. "But I look nine."

The boy slept beside Jacob most of the night before the mother came to get him. Jacob woke several times (kicked awake), finally finding the boy's feet in his lap, but later finding the boy gone. Light was beginning to come and he recognized more clearly the trees and fields that moved by. And as they passed rows of sugar cane, Jacob wished to step down and cut stalks from a summer field. As a boy, he worked one summer in Alabama and split the cane stalk, watching the place where moisture would appear. Each thin, firm stalk held in its wooden case a sweet pithy substance and a texture that would last. Nothing seemed so noble to him then as sugar cane, so pleasurable to carry in his hand. The stalks now were cut and broken flat for winter. Jacob raised his hand to greet the day, his fingers ranged long and thin with knuckles that stuck out hard like bolts. The day came up over the slow fields, and for a while when the light was right, Jacob could see both the trees outside and the reflection of the couple asleep across the aisle, not by looking at the reflection or the trees directly, but looking at some point further out that allowed him both visions.

"You coming?" Jacob's sister called to him from the house. She had fixed a big meal for his arrival and leaned from the porch to find him. "You coming, Jake?" Annie looked old to Jacob, finally old, her arms pushing out like leavened bread. Her hair, a dull gray, uncolored, uncut, was pulled into a tight, high knot. But she moved with an agility that belonged to her youth, and Jacob still loved to look at her.

Sweetwater lay nestled in a valley surrounded by high mountains and hills. A river snaked through the valley as though for years it had been looking for a way out. Jacob had walked into the field behind his sister's house. Annie's house was beside the river. It had been the house where Jacob grew up. He knew of no one anymore who, when they returned home, returned to their actual home. The house itself was modest, but each window faced a splendid countryside, a mountain range with foothills blue or purple depending on the distance, and a river where barges hauled coal from Virginia mines. Annie raised her children in this house and now brought grandchildren to let them learn what they could from roaming the hills by day and watching the mountains at night.

"Dinner's getting cold," Annie called again. She shaded her eyes to see him. Jacob waved, knowing she would not see, but would notice a wave, knowing too that her dinner was a long way from being cold.

Jacob walked across the field toward her house, her voice. He could see the river both here at Annie's house and farther off a thin strip he knew was water. Mountains rose up from that strip, large and wide, as though they had been planted there.

He stumbled, then lifted what he stumbled on: a bone of an animal, two feet long, two-and-a-half feet maybe, with a grand old knob at either end. The knob (knee? shoulder?) begged his touch and he rested one hand on top of it. It seemed a small head in his palm and he wondered about the size of an animal whose joints could be as large as this. He searched, scanning for more evidence, something that would tell him he had stumbled across an ice age beast, an animal that ate nothing but berries or leaves and weighed one hundred thousand pounds, whose cry was at once both high and deep and similar to what lay inside Jacob's own head on days he couldn't hold it down. He laid the bone beside the tree, deciding it was a cowbone, nothing more, though not really deciding, just leaving it in this way.

He pressed the back of his neck. It ached with the long ride here. He had spent one whole night and most of today on the train. As he looked down, he noticed, as though suddenly, how his clothes appeared unkempt. He buttoned one button higher on his shirt and hoped it made a difference.

When he walked into the house, he could hear Annie at the stove, as she asked why people didn't come to dinner when they were called, asking no one in particular, the stove. Jacob spoke to Albert, her husband. He waited at the table in the wheelchair he had been bound to since a young man. Albert asked how Molly was and said he wished she could have come with Jacob. Jacob told him she might come for a weekend. Annie set a large pot in the middle of the table and Albert lifted the lid. He praised the cut carrots and sizable potatoes wreathed against the dark meat. They took large helpings of everything.

Often at night, Jacob pretended to return to Sweetwater and find that what was written in the clipping was only a dream.

7

Not that he dreamed of it anymore, but by lying awake he pretended to dream.

It all happened within a few moments: Jacob entering his brother's house, hearing a shot, and even before he heard it his infallible intuition announced *Something will happen here* or *I will be changed*. Incumbent upon him was some nameless happening.

Then as he turned over in bed, he would pretend Drue was still alive, that he would meet his brother on the street or that Drue would come to visit Jacob. And at those times he gave to Drue a life, one full of children, a wife and job. And in that near-sleep wish-state, Jacob even talked with Drue, asked whatever came to mind. But the difficult part to pretend or even to imagine was his brother at the age he would be now, sixty-four. He could not bring up the image, aged and gray. The brother he talked to and pretended alive was always twenty-three, though Jacob himself grew older, older than his older brother. Sometimes though he had a memory of them both as children, something they did, some argument, and those memories were easier and left him feeling freer from guilt.

For the times that he dreamed, leaving Drue on the floor in the hallway of the house, he could smell the odor of burning, and he would call out Drue's name, loudly, in a loud voice, Drue, Dru-u-ue, drawing it out to a thin screech as it had been drawn out inside him over the years. The noise always ended in an explicable high pitch. And to Molly or anyone who heard it late at night (the children, a guest, anybody), it made all surfaces seem black and watery, the noise itself becoming an impregnable shadow. So Molly would say, "Wake up, Jake. You're having a nightmare," but the next morning she always pretended not to know what it was about.

When Molly took Jacob to the train station she had packed his bag to stay for several weeks. There would be a hunting

8

trip, so she included his gear. Some of it lay loose around his bag and she cautioned him to keep up with it.

"You look like a child," she told him, "a worried child."

Jacob handed her the clipping, yellow and brittle, from the *Sweetwater Sentinel* which was now called the *Herald*. Molly knew this clipping, knew all about it, and in fact had saved a copy for herself in a drawer beside her bed. When she handed the clipping back to Jacob, he gave her something else, a letter. It was the one from Callie.

"She must be close to a hundred years old by now," said Molly, looking to the scratchy signature. "What does she say?" She strained to read, but found the arthritic writing too difficult to make out.

Jacob said that he didn't know exactly, then looked to Molly as though he should have to say no more. He folded the letter and clipping and slipped it into his inside jacket pocket.

Molly didn't speak too quickly of what they had not spoken of in so many years. After a few moments, she asked, "What is it?" So Jacob decided to tell her. Here. In this place where people wandered and drank Cokes and spoke irritably to each other. In this public place he told Molly what he had not told her before. His words fell on her like hard rain, seeping deep enough for her to hear, and Jacob hoped, forgive.

"I went to Drue's house that night," Jacob began.

"Whose?" Molly thought he was confused.

"Drue's. Drue's house." Jacob's expression looked as though someone had just given him that information. "When I got there everything was dark, so I thought he had gone to sleep, probably on the sofa, and lay there still. I called out, hoped to wake him. I wanted to apologize. I had been angry with him and I think I even hated him." He looked to Molly. Molly needed no reminding. She nodded to tell him she remembered. Then Jacob pointed to the floor as though the floor would be included in what he had to tell. They both looked down.

"But as I went into the hallway, I noticed a lamp in the

9

back room and I could see all the way down the hall like it was a tunnel. The kitchen window had a reflection, a lamp was on back there and there was firelight from the room where Drue was. It was reflected in the window, so that the glass seemed yellow.

"I heard scuffling and something bumping into furniture, so I stopped before I could see into the room. I thought at first that Drue's dog was tearing at something, playing. I looked to the gun case beside the door. It was already open. One of the revolvers Drue kept clean and ready to fire was gone. I picked up the other one. I called out *Drue* before going farther in and when I did a gun went off somewhere in the house. I knew I didn't do it, or thought I didn't. I don't remember when I put the gun down. I could still hear noises, no words. Drue didn't answer my call, and it was like my calling out had fired the shot. I wanted to ask what was happening and have someone stand up and explain to me what to do. I hoped it would be easy." Jacob shifted in his seat. Molly didn't move.

"I stayed in the hallway. I don't know how long. Not long, I think. I could see only partway into the room. I remember fire and shadows growing larger on the opposite wall. So I knew at some point that the fire was out of hand, though I didn't know how it started. It was burning the room, the house. But it was so fast, all of it so fast.

"I heard another noise, a door slam, something. Then I saw, saw Drue coming toward me. His mouth was open as though he wanted to sing. But no sound came. There was only the sound burning makes—a soft, hissing, swishing sound that came from behind him, though not far behind. Drue's clothes had caught fire and he was trying to run, to run." Jacob stopped his telling here, remembering though not saying how Drue's hair, clothes, everything went upward, burning him in the way fire burns a piece of paper, holding it up. How Drue's face was black on one side, so that he looked like a tragic-comic mask used to emblem a play, and the singing

10

mouth turned into a smile that stayed or else contorted itself on the blackened side.

"When Drue fell," Jacob told, "he fell heavy like a sack of grain. I knew he was dead then." Jacob looked up and leaned back now, through with the worst; but then he leaned forward again almost parallel to the floor and Molly thought that the worst was still to come. "He had come around the corner, hearing my voice, I guess." The heels of Jacob's hands pressed against his temples. "I left, right then I left and I ran down the hill to my car, not even trying to drag him out." Jacob turned to Molly as though he had asked a question and she would tell him now why he had acted in that way. Molly looked up but not at him. "And I thought then, Molly, I really thought then that I might wake up and be home, having only dreamed it all. I thought I would come and tell you and you would laugh or comfort me."

Molly sought a way to comfort him, not reaching for his arm or hand or even making a remark as she would have done years ago but which would not be adequate now. She stayed distant, listening, saying, "Jacob, that was a long time ago. You've carried it longer than maybe you should." And she looked around to the people walking in the station and wondered why Jacob had chosen, after all these years of silence, this place to say what he needed to say now. Then she repeated that he had carried it too long, saying it in a way that gave only a little weight, letting it lay there in the conversation that was directed by him. And her words had the effect of a touch or a pat.

It relieved him some, because he agreed he had done that, carried it long and hard. So Molly knew she had said the right thing, because when someone agrees at a time like that, they're usually relieved, but if the wrong thing has been said and relief does not come that person grows silent or else begins to defend himself.

"I went home," Jacob started again. "Mother was up and

she called out, but she didn't see my face." Molly could see Jacob's face. His eyes, the color of smoke, held a pearliness like ice and sometimes when she looked at him it was the only thing she recognized anymore. "When I went upstairs, I looked in the mirror," Jacob lifted his face to the ceiling of the station house, "just to see how I had changed. And Molly," and he turned to tell her something, not with the grief and distress he had shown before, but with the expression of someone telling a fabulous secret. "I looked then the way I look now. That night showed me for a few moments how I would age. Put the years on me, as though I had missed them or wouldn't have them. But I have, and the only thing about it is that the face I have today is the face that looked back at me that night when I was nineteen years old." Molly didn't know what to say, but she knew the telling was over.

It did not take long that night, the space of a couple of hours maybe, for word to get back to the Bechner home that Drue had burned, that a blaze had caught the curtains that reached all the way to the ceiling and fire had rushed quickly through the hallway. That Drue himself must have been asleep, and awakened to the fire too late, his clothes catching. He tried to run, but had fallen before reaching the door. He had not gotten up.

"Mrs. Bechner?" the officer asked as he entered their house. They waited in the living room: Jacob, his father, his mother, and Annie. "Mr. Bechner?" Karl Bechner nodded. "I guess you've already heard." They all nodded.

"We heard he was dead. Drue was dead." His mother wished to have it refuted.

"Yes."

"A fire."

"Yes."

"How did it start?" Jacob asked. No one mentioned the gunshot. Jacob waited to hear as he sat in the living room that night with his astonished mother and his drunken father, and Annie. He waited to hear that the autopsy told how Drue had been shot, because Jacob had heard it. And he wondered for years if the shot he heard was not a real shot, but just something set off in his own mind that made him wonder what he was capable of.

It was not mentioned, never mentioned, so Jacob did not mention it either. Except on those nights when he called out, ending in his thin wail. And coming back to Sweetwater now, he wondered if this was something Callie could tell him about. He hoped it was.

It was almost time to board the train. They could hear the man calling "All Aboard" in a voice that you couldn't tell what he was saying, but knew by the inflection what he meant. Molly bought them each some ice cream in small cups and they ate as they walked along. She talked of how Jacob would enjoy the hunting trip and she named people to tell hello, and to tell Callie hello. When Jacob kissed her good-bye he thought her eyes looked the way a young girl's eyes look when she tells the boy she loves good-bye and will not see him for several months. And Jacob felt lucky to have her.

Molly handed him a sack of apples and walnuts. As the train pulled out, Jacob could see her standing on the platform. It seemed as though she was the one moving away. He could see her straining, lifting her whole head and body as a boy would or a bird. So he watched, until the last vestige of her and the platform fell out of sight, dropping finally over the edge of the horizon as a ship might do.

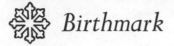 *Birthmark*

"We won't find it here. Not here," Drue told Jacob.
Drue was already fifteen, and though Jacob was only eleven he was taller and weighed more. They looked for a place to fish, but Drue kept arguing or wanting to fight. He jumped in front of Jacob in the road and said, "Fight." He held up both fists.

"I don't want to." Jacob brushed Drue aside with his arm.

Drue jabbed at him a few times. He had just learned the art of fighting from his friends and wanted to practice on Jacob. "You scared?" Then he hit Jacob's mouth. Jacob decked him with one blow. Drue lay on the ground holding his jaw.

"Okay." Drue got up and gripped his feet to the ground as if he had claws. "Again."

Again Jacob's fist caught Drue's jaw to the air, his feet rising upward. He landed, same spot.

"Okay," he said more slowly, as though the first lesson had gone well, but now was over. He looked around for some other way to prove himself.

"Let's race to the creek, the rest of the way." He started to run. "Now. Go." So they raced. Drue won. Then they raced again to where Hawley's Creek spilled into the river, then further down to a place called Reeker's Point.

It was Saturday. A May sun beat down on them as they walked to the river's rapids. It had rained for three days

14

straight and they wanted to see how high the river was. They brought fishing gear, but would not be bound to fishing if they could think of something better.

They stopped at Reeker's Point. A man named Reeker drowned making his way down the rapids, but that was forty years ago, and whenever Drue mentioned to Jacob that they should try the rapids, Jacob said no. Then Drue always mentioned how they were not as bad now as they were forty years ago when that man named Reeker drowned.

A large rubber raft lay beneath some branches. Drue checked it for holes by attempting to dunk it. "It's good," he said.

"You sure?" Jacob looked around to see if the owner of the raft might return. He knew Drue wanted to take it. Drue had been in trouble before for taking things. In fact, the last time was only a few weeks ago. He and two friends stole cigarettes from Locke's Store. It was night and they broke a window and climbed in. They didn't take any money or even anything to eat, but were caught with several packs of cigarettes that had not been opened. Nobody would've known Drue had done it if he hadn't dropped his fish hook on Ruben Locke's floor. Drue had a fish hook that he wore all the time on his jacket. It got to be his trademark: that hook hanging there near his collar. His mother said she thought he dropped the fish hook on purpose and that he wanted to get caught, because the hook was almost impossible to get out and whenever she cleaned his jacket, Drue had to take it out for her.

Nothing much was done to the boys. A reprimand from the court and from Ruben Locke. A tongue lashing from Callie. A firm slap by his father and, worst, silence from his mother. But that wasn't all of it. Drue was required to return the cigarettes, make an apology. He did, though the other boys did not come with him. But Jacob went with him. Jacob said later how Drue's teeth were clenched as he spoke apologies. Ruben

15

Locke took those words, expecting no more than that. Callie, who was Ruben's wife, offered doughnuts and Jacob accepted. Drue said no and left. Jacob ate the doughnuts that would have been Drue's.

"Sure. Sure. It's fine." Drue dunked the raft again, or rather tried. It was sturdy. He climbed in and steadied it for Jacob. The oars lay in the middle side by side. They ignored the river rising on the banks and, further down, the rocks and foam. As they pushed away from the bank, the force of the water started them downstream. The river was faster than they imagined. Debris rode along the top and Jacob could see eddies and whirlpools and one log carried along at surprising speed.

Soon the raft was moving of its own volition and Jacob wondered if the oaring did anything to affect their course, or if it merely gave a person something to do in the middle of all the roar and noise. Whichever he decided, he continued to work against the current until they both fell onto their knees in the bottom of the raft, trying to keep from falling out.

They worked without talking. Their excitement was the kind that was overlaid with fear and warns the mind to stay in control. Jacob thought of how they would rest on the bank when it was over. He thought too of the fishing gear they had left behind and how someone would probably take it, a fair swap. His mother would be angry that they had lost their new poles and tackle box.

There were places along the river where the water dropped off twenty, sometimes fifty feet. The boys saw such a place ahead of them, and tried to paddle to shore. It was no use.

"We're going over," Drue yelled. But Drue went under. The water completely covered his head and oar, his head staying under such a long time that Jacob felt helpless to find him, or even to know where to extend his own oar. It seemed hours before Drue bobbed up, his arms working with the steadiness of a paddle wheel. It would be years later, when Jacob would stand in the hallway, in that same paralyzed way,

16

waiting for Drue's arms to work, for his head to bob up again like that day at the river.

Finally, Jacob did extend his oar to pull Drue into the boat. Neither of them spoke. The water subsided and let them coast, so they lay back awhile until Jacob said, "Look. It's full of holes." Drue leaned to see tiny gashes where rocks had cut. The water seeped in.

They guided themselves to the nearest clearing on the bank, then pulled the raft out of sight and fell onto the ground, not so much from exhaustion as from not wanting to admit they didn't know where they were.

Drue spoke first. "Fastest ride I ever had."

"Me too."

Drue pulled a blade of grass and began to suck on it. Jacob did the same.

"When we went over the big falls," said Jacob, "I thought you were gone. I couldn't see you anywhere."

"Naw. I just went under." Drue turned to lie on his stomach. "I'll tell you though, it did seem I was gonna drown."

"I saw your paddle come up first, then your head."

"Yeah." They were silent, thinking, sucking on their grass. "What would you have done though, if I hadn't?"

"If you hadn't come up?"

"Yeah."

"I would've gone in after you. Yeah, I would've jumped in, pulled you up." And Jacob meant it.

"It probably would've gotten both of us," said Drue, looking at the water. Then he said, "Let's go," and jumped up to get his bearings, making a decision about which way to walk and motioning for Jacob to follow. They walked awhile without saying anything, then Drue asked Jacob a question, but it was one that he wanted to be asked himself.

"What would you want most?" Drue said. "I mean, if you could have anything at all, what would you want?"

Jacob leaped ahead to kick at a can, then some rocks. "I

17

don't know." He had thought of one thing, but didn't want to say it. "What do *you* want?"

"Hannah Zandowski." Drue had not hesitated.

"Who?"

"You've seen Hannah, haven't you. I mean since Christmas?"

"Sure. I guess so. Why?"

"She grew a set of big ones. Seems like they popped out overnight. I don't know. She just came back with her blouses chock full of tit."

Jacob forgot what his own answer would have been. "They're not real," he said.

"They *are*." Drue's expression was one of someone who had been personally insulted. "Freddy Finney has had his hands on them. He's telling everybody they're real."

"Well, I heard something else."

"What?"

"That Hannah made a deal with Freddy that if he'd tell everybody they were real, she'd say he'd touched her."

"Some deal."

"It was for Freddy. He's in *my* grade."

Drue picked up a stick and broke it, but kept walking. "Anyway," he said, but he didn't finish. Instead he began to look around to see if he could recognize where they were. An old pumphouse stood in the middle of a field and Drue pointed. "See that pumphouse? I think I know where we are now."

But Jacob couldn't stop picturing Hannah, stuffing handkerchiefs inside her brassiere. And the bosom they all imagined beneath her blouse was only the small bump that was there before Christmas. There had been no miraculous swelling during the Advent season.

"What's it for?" Jacob had turned toward the pumphouse.

"They don't use it now. They used to. To put out fires."

"Out here?"

"Yeah. Before you were born there was a Live Bear Show that came to town every fall. A woman named Hattie ran it.

18

Never knew her last name. Just Hattie. There was a fire hose and a pump for the fire department." They walked toward the pumphouse, so Drue could show Jacob.

"The hose wrapped around the pump in a way that made it look like a snake, and whenever I lifted it I was surprised at how heavy it was." Jacob pictured a great, thick, fibrous snake as long as a fire hose. "I can only remember the fire department using it twice. Once when a brush fire took half these woods," and he pointed to the woods on the right, "and once for Hattie.

"I was almost four when Mama took me on the last day to see the show. Annie never liked to go, and Mama was big with you." Drue pointed to his stomach to indicate pregnancy. "We walked underneath the paper streamers that said HATTIE'S LIVE BEAR SHOW, and below that 'Also Alligators and Rides.'

"I knew what to expect because I had been before, and as I walked in I asked Mama if I could have a cherry smash *and* cotton candy, because usually I got only one, but I always tried for both. I said I wanted it first, and we started toward the concession stand when the machine with all the rides hooked to it began to spit. Sparks flew all over like fireworks. Later, people said they thought it *was* fireworks and that maybe Hattie had added something new to her show. But the sparks landed on the tent where the bear show was and on the awning of the concession stand and when the fires flared up, people knew.

"But there was an alligator that I mentioned." Jacob nodded to let him know he remembered. Drue continued. They had left the pumphouse and were walking toward home. "People could touch the alligator because they had drugged him into a deep sleep, and people for years had let even their smallest kids touch him. They even lifted his mouth and touched his teeth. His teeth were dark yellow, though sharp. And his breath was sharp too." Jacob chuckled.

"Some people would say he was dead or stuffed, and when

19

they did that, the keeper would make him move a little, so they would know he was alive. Because it wouldn't mean a thing to touch a dead one." Drue paused and when he spoke again his voice left his mouth as if he were a radio.

"When the machines began to spit, a little girl was touching the alligator. She had just leaned to him wanting to see his mouth and teeth, but the fireworks brought the animal up out of his sleep to find the little girl's arm at his mouth. And he rallied himself up to take one quick swipe, like a pair of scissors," Drue knifed his hands in the air, "slicing her arm and taking part of her dress with him. Then he went back again to his sleep.

"That mother screamed to high heaven and she held the little girl up over her head like she was part of the show and needed applauding. Lots of people clapped and the girl looked down at her own arm. It hung ragged and loose and looked just like part of her dress. Then she passed out. Mama ran to them and told me to hold on to her skirt and not let go.

"The fires burned wherever sparks hit. They came up everywhere. The tent burned full force, and the awning." Jacob watched Drue with a dumb admiration. "Mama carried the little girl and told her mother to follow. I ran behind and wondered if I would still get to buy the cherry smash *and* the cotton candy, but suspecting I wouldn't.

"The people backed away from the heat, though at the same time they were drawn to it. They called to people they knew, trying to make sure someone they loved was not caught by the flames.

"The bears, two of them, dressed in tiny ballerina skirts that stuck out from their middles and a lei of flowers around their necks, didn't stand now, but were on all fours running from the tent and scattering the people like they were beads. Hattie never came out of the tent. They found her and knew it was her by the gold earrings and the silver brocade shoes

20

she had worn ever since she had been coming to Sweetwater.

"Hattie was in her fifties, Mama said. There were stories about her. She danced naked for the king of France, for one. There was another story about how she married and had two children before she decided she wanted a carnival life (which she herself admitted was not all as glamorous and easy as it appeared). But it was the show business she loved, and it never got out of her blood.

"No one said what happened to her family or where they were, so when it came time to bury Hattie, the funeral was held by the town. It was the only time the town performed something for Hattie, and everybody thought that was kind of nice."

Drue stopped and Jacob wondered if that was the end, then Drue said, "That little girl's living over in Knoxville. She got to where she loved to tell the story of her arm, because it didn't look too bad. I think she played it for all it was worth."

Jacob turned to see if he was through now.

"Is that true?" Jacob asked, wondering why he hadn't heard this before.

"Every bit of it."

But Jacob didn't know, and when they got home and his mother was through fussing about the poles and tackle box and how late they were, Jacob asked if she had ever heard of Hattie's Live Bear Show. She said Yes, that Drue had been with her when it burned down. "And I was pregnant with you." She touched her stomach just as Drue had touched his own. "And wasn't that awful about that little girl," she said, "but she seems to be all right now."

But Jacob didn't see how anybody could be all right after that.

Drue had a birthmark. Not one that changed the shape of his face, not one that was swollen. But one that was dark, a dark purple that scattered over the lower half of one of his

21

cheeks. Still, even with that, he was handsome. The girls, rather than ignoring it or making fun of it, would ask him about it, as if he had been given some privilege they didn't understand. They asked if it bothered him, one asked if it hurt. Drue always pretended that he had forgotten all about it, saying, "Oh, yes. That. No, it doesn't bother me at all," or "It doesn't hurt at all," and the girls would leave smiling.

But Jacob would see Drue in the mornings as he stood in front of the bathroom mirror, inspecting his dark place, looking at it closely as if he thought he might think of a way to take the whole ferocious sight off, remove it for good. And there were times, late at night, when Jacob heard Drue talking to their father and mother. He was upset, frustrated with his mother's answer and his father's attempt to lie.

Sarah would say, "There's nothing we can do. You know that. We've told you, Drue." His father told him that as he grew older the mark would lessen, become smaller or lighter in color so that it would hardly be noticed. Then their voices would finally turn to anger. "Drue, this is silly," they told him. "It's late." And they would tell him what a good-looking boy he was and how everyone thought that. So Drue would go back to bed.

It was true. Drue was good-looking. He had thick blond hair and dark brown eyes, and though he wasn't big, his frame was wiry and strong, and girls were especially drawn to his secretive personality.

"Go on to bed now," his mother told him as she opened the door to their bedroom. She watched as Drue climbed into bed, then closed the door. Jacob could hear Drue with his face in the pillow, his sounds going hard into it. They shared a room until Jacob was twelve. One night during one of these episodes, Jacob wondered if there was something he could do, so he said Drue's name out loud and Drue stopped his sound, growing as still as he could, not even moving his face from the pillow. Jacob did not say anything else.

22

The next morning Drue said, "You talked in your sleep last night."

"I did? What'd I say?"

"I don't know. Something." And Jacob noticed that Drue had his hand over a portion of the mark, holding it lightly as though he had been burned and was feeling to see how it was.

Jacob slept late the next day and stayed around the house all afternoon, deciding not to go into town as he had planned. "You're not going in today?" Annie asked him.

"No. Tomorrow," he said and she thought he was just tired. She told him that her grandchildren were coming over after dinner, and sliced tomatoes for the dinner table. The tomatoes were fresh from her garden and Annie was proud that her vines produced this late into fall.

"I was fifteen the year I planted my first tomatoes," Annie said. "Tomatoes, lettuce, zinnias, and marigolds." She listed these in order of importance.

But that was the year too that their father began to spend most of his time drunk. Annie would return home from school to find him outstretched on the couch, lying in a position of languorous dissipation, not comfort.

"Annie," he said, upon hearing her come in, "my dear."

Annie said What, but she knew when he said "my dear" that he wanted her to do something. His mind had deepened the past year into a screen full of holes, and his body, which was never athletic, was now soft and shaky and at times unmanageable.

"Annie," he said, "my drink is over there," and he pointed to the other side of the room where there was a table. But there was no drink there and Annie wondered if he meant for her to make one for him. She didn't know how to do it.

Then he fell suddenly off the couch. He wasn't trying to get up, but just unconsciously rolled off and the loud thump he made without saying anything, made Annie call out to him. She called loud, as if she thought he was in another room.

23

When he didn't answer, it occurred to her he might be dead.

"He's dead," Annie said to no one, but told it for years, saying, "And I said to myself, only I said it out loud, 'He's dead.' I said it over and over. But mother came in and said 'No, he's not, dear,' because she had seen this before. She called Drue and Jacob to help her lift him onto the couch. She left him there and gave us dinner."

Later, when her mother told them good night she said "Annie, are you okay?" and Annie told her she was, but started to cry, because she thought her father was actually dead and that her mother was protecting them from knowing the truth. So her mother took her downstairs and helped to put cold towels on Karl's face and chest until he revived. When he woke, he said "Annie," but didn't remember anything about asking for a drink. He almost didn't remember Annie, because he said her name in such a slow way, she thought he might be guessing at it. Her mother brought coffee and he drank it without asking for anything else. Then she said, "Karl, you nearly scared this girl to death," and Annie agreed. He said he was sorry and sipped his coffee, but he didn't look up at Annie, or anybody.

That was the beginning of years that would be too difficult to remember, so that Annie remembered the early years with her father, trying not to think of the later ones.

And that was the year too that Annie put away her dollhouse. The one that Karl made for her. In that house was the predictable family: a mother figure with ear-length hair that turned under and a pink-dotted dress that she wore all the years that Annie had the house. A father figure in a yellow shirt and light blue pants that got rubbed off with handling so that he looked finally as if he always wore a white suit. A boy figure holding a ball and a girl figure with a pocketbook. One small dog with his legs spread slightly apart to make him stand easily. There was another dog and a cat painted on the wall of the living room, sleeping next to a fireplace that burned both summer and winter.

The kitchen of the dollhouse had items on the counters. Meals included two tiny steaks that looked only partially cooked, a small bottle of milk, a basket of cherries that were very small and were glued together to stay inside the basket, never to be lost or eaten. There was also in the kitchen an item which Annie added and which gave the kitchen a bizarre look. It was a regular size egg, taken from their own kitchen, and was larger than either of the parent figures, larger than the table where they sat and the door which went out onto the veranda. It was also larger than the veranda.

And at times, Jacob brought back to mind those Christmases with socks lined up on the mantel that made their family seem stronger than it was, and sometimes without really bringing it to his mind, he would think of the giant egg.

Promised Something Big

Annie offered second helpings to both men before clearing the table. She then placed a quart of ice cream out to soften.

"Verna's bringing her two children over in a little while," she told Jacob. Jacob couldn't picture Verna, couldn't remember in his mind's eye which one of Annie's children she was. It had been years since he had seen any of them.

"We take care of them sometimes on weekends." Albert steered his wheelchair to look out the window. He wore a thick plaid shirt and his hair was black and curly. He seemed younger than Annie. "But tonight's Ty's birthday. He's seven." He kept his hands propped on each wheel, his arms stuck out like a cricket's.

Annie put the cake with candles on the table. She did not look so old, really, only six years older than Jacob. But still, she was older than Jacob ever thought she could be. As she leaned to put the cake in the middle of the table, Jacob could see down the front of her dress. He knew more about his sister than he should know.

He had hidden in her closet once, planning to scare her when she returned home from school. That was when he was eight, and she was fourteen. The closet door lay cracked open and he could see her come in and stand before the mirror, not brushing her hair or drawing on lipstick. She stretched herself slowly, and Jacob strained to see if anyone had come into the room, because it seemed as though Annie thought she was being watched, or wanted to be watched.

Then she pulled down her skirt, removing it in the mirror and she pushed with both hands between her legs, rubbing against her underpants. Her hips moved against her fingers, pushing in a way that Jacob thought must be hurting her. He tried to think of something else. He was kneeling on Annie's Sunday shoes, which were patent leather and stuck to his legs. And he looked to see if he could scoot over, but the closet was dark and he could see no empty space to put his knees. When he looked up again, Annie had moved to the bed and he couldn't see her anymore. When she was through, she put her skirt back on. Jacob could see that her face was flushed and how the ribbing of the bedspread had made its imprint on her cheek. She tucked in her blouse and went downstairs.

Jacob never forgot the incident. It had been more erotic to him than anything he would see in his adult life, until Molly, the first time he touched her. And when he did, she pushed against his hand the way Annie had pushed against her own fingertips, throwing her head back at the same time, as if some great button had been found that jerked at her body like puppet strings.

"Last year the pond froze hard," Annie told Jacob, as though Jacob had not been away for seven years, as though he knew all the years when it froze only partly. "But not to skate on." She straightened the candles and though she was talking to Jacob she did not look at him, instead she went to stand behind Albert who waited at the window. Albert looked to see what Annie would tell. "Last winter," said Annie, "Verna's youngest fell in. They didn't find him 'til spring."

Jacob remembered Verna now: Annie and Albert's middle child. Annie had had five children, but Verna had been the quiet one, unassuming; but who, at sixteen, had run off with a

27

man twice her age and stayed gone for years, returning finally with three children and no husband. Now one child gone. Jacob remembered the call to Virginia last January, saying that Jonathan had fallen through the ice, but they couldn't find him, then they found him. And Jacob remembered it with all the force with which he had heard it that day.

Annie kept saying that this was the reason she never allowed anyone to go to the pond in winter, challenging the arguments that the pond was frozen "clear through," by saying there was no way to know for sure.

"Somebody's here," said Annie as they heard a car pull into the driveway. Annie took off her apron and pushed at her hair on the way to the door. A car door slammed. In moments children were in the house. Jacob shook hands with the seven-year-old boy, who approached him directly and showed him a new pocket knife in a leather sheath. The girl was older by a few years. She was eleven maybe. She didn't come to Jacob directly, but stood back, circling the kitchen before she spoke. Her hair was very blond and hung to her shoulders. She had long bangs cut straight across her forehead, and her face had the beauty of an older woman. Annie smiled, showing Jacob the children as though she had promised something big and kept her promise. When Verna came in, Jacob noticed she carried a new baby that no one had mentioned.

Verna's husband was in jail in Illinois. She went to see him each spring but this past year when young Jonathan fell through the ice in January and could not be found, Verna went to Illinois. She was still married and still wore her ring. She came back in March carrying his child.

Jonathan was found at the end of March. By then, Verna knew she was pregnant, or pretty well knew it. When she stood at the bank of the river that gave her her pond, she watched the men drag it with a wide net; and she saw them pulling up the limp half-gone body of three-year-old Jonathan, bringing to the surface his clothes that lay draped as though they had been thrown haphazardly on top of him.

Verna stood and saw Jonathan lifted, put on the ground, and she could not help but touch her own belly, feeling the child there in her own water—one child lifted dead from a deep pond, put on the ground, then into the ground and this new one emerging live in her own water, not able to drown, but fed by it. And as she watched, her mind grew hard and she thought he looked like no one she'd ever seen.

Verna showed her new child to Jacob, holding it out so he could see its large healthy size. Jacob didn't want to hold it, because he felt uncomfortable with babies that small, never knowing what to say or how to act without seeming foolish. Verna propped him again on her shoulder, his cheeks pressed loose and slack. He looked only a few weeks old.

Verna's hair was almost red, not dyed or tinted or even very well cared-for, but a dark auburn color that complemented her white freckled skin.

"What's your name?" Jacob asked the loose-mouthed baby itself.

Verna said, "We've named him Joseph." It was the name Jacob had chosen for his oldest son. Jacob thought of his own son, dead now, and didn't want to hear anyone named that name. But he said how nice that was.

Albert spoke to the little girl. She seemed to want to tell Albert about something that had happened. He patted her back. The girl circled the room again.

"Did you speak to Jacob?" Annie asked the girl. The asking irritated.

"I *will*."

Jacob suggested they have some cake.

The little girl stood close to Albert as they sang "Happy Birthday." Jacob wondered if she remembered her own father. She had not seen him in four years. None of the children had really known him, but they knew their mother, or thought they did. Though they didn't know why she went off to Illinois each spring, regular as the season. And they didn't know why their father had gone to jail.

But this past spring Verna went to Illinois and came back carrying this child. Their brother fell through the ice in January, Verna went to Illinois, and now it was November and a new brother was here, and the children fought in ways worse than they ever had.

"I get to sleep in the upstairs room," the girl said. She stood behind Jacob, now eating cake with her fingers.

"No." Ty had not remembered to say it first, hardly ever remembered. "I want that room."

"Ty gets the cake and presents," Annie handled the disagreement as though she expected it, "so you" and she pointed to the girl, "get to sleep in the upstairs room." It was settled.

Ty showed his knife again to Jacob. Jacob took it, turned it over in his hands and tried to think of more to say about it. "It's like the ones the Indians used to have." Ty was pleased and began to tell Jacob about a circus that would arrive for the weekend.

When Verna left, Joseph was again asleep on her shoulder. She told the children she would pick them up at noon the next day. Jacob looked to the little girl and realized he didn't even know her name.

The little girl's name was Cedar. She was ten and dressed as boyishly as she could. She told her name to Jacob, then said, "Like the tree," with a certain acerbity. She tried always to say it before a grown-up's eyes glazed over with the effort to think of something clever to say, which was never directed at her but rather for the amusement of other adults standing around. "Like the tree," she would say, but Jacob could tell, even though her mouth was set in a hard, straight line, that she liked her name.

"Both children were home," Annie told Jacob. She had sent the children to play for a while before going to bed. Albert had gone to his room. They had finished cake and ice cream and Annie washed the dishes, placed them into the drainer. "Both of them were home and helped Verna have that baby. They called me, but I knew from what they described that I would not get there in time, so I called the hospital and they sent an ambulance to Verna's house. Then I went over myself. When I got there, both children were helping."

Jacob tried to picture it. "How?"

"I could hear Verna giving instructions. When I opened the bedroom door I saw Ty holding up his mother's knees, pushing on them so she couldn't straighten them. Verna saying, 'Hold them up, Ty. Hold them.' Cedar stood at the end of the bed. The baby's head and shoulders were out and Cedar held that head like a basketball player taking the ball for a free throw. Then the rest of the baby came out and I reached to catch it, because Cedar had only the head. The ambulance was there by then, the doctor cut the cord, then cleaned the baby's mouth." Annie placed the last plate into the drainer and sat down. "Ty was still holding his mother's knees, her legs. I told him that he could let go and when he did, that was the moment of the baby's first cry. And Ty looked as though he thought the cry had something to do with the release of his mother's legs."

There was one plate with a small amount of cake left. Annie decided to leave it, let people pick the rest with their fingers until it was gone. She called to tell the children good night and asked Jacob to put them to bed for her, said that she was tired. She went to the bedroom off the kitchen where Albert was. Annie called "Albert" before entering the room. When she opened the door, Jacob could see Albert in the bed, reading. He wondered what their life had been like.

Then he heard the children arguing. They ran downstairs to the kitchen.

"Mama *said*." Ty's voice had found tears. He was accustomed to taking Cedar's harassment, but this time Cedar roused him.

"No," Cedar's voice sounded adult, authoritative beyond all questioning. "What she *meant* was," and she paused here, "that you could not have more cake until *tomorrow*."

"Mama said I could have another piece before I went to bed." He saw Jacob. "Cedar said I couldn't have any cake."

"Sure you can."

"What I *meant* was," Cedar explained, "that he should not have *too much cake*." She turned on her heels to go back upstairs, but tossed her head once before leaving. "It makes him sick."

"No. It does not."

But Cedar had already left the room.

Jacob followed Ty upstairs to tell him good night. There were crumbs in his bed and Ty asked Jacob to help him get them out and then wanted to be tucked in. As he climbed between the sheets, he told Jacob where to tighten the covers so the pressure would feel right. He lay flat with his arms straight at his side and the covers pulled up to his neck. His body looked as though he might sleep forever, but his face was far from sleep.

"There's a circus coming tomorrow," Ty had already told Jacob this, but told it again. "Last year we went." He jumped from the bed, mobbing Jacob with the covers. He found two pennants and some souvenirs bought at last year's circus. "They have elephants that do tricks, and when they poop, a man comes and cleans it up with a wheelbarrow."

"Guess you'd have to."

"It's coming tomorrow." This last statement seemed to border on being a question.

"Well, now."

"Me and Cedar want to go." He had jumped back into bed. Jacob tried to tuck the covers in again. Ty's head on the pillow was cocked and expectant and Jacob saw in him a facial quality that had been passed down, an expression, not so much an imitation of features as a familiarity around the forehead and eyes that he wore like a band, an expression achieved only through inheritance.

"You want to take us?" Ty asked, the question finally coming.

"Well, sure," said Jacob. And Ty's face showed everything.

In the highest upstairs room, Cedar said she didn't need to be tucked in, but that Jacob could if he wanted to. Jacob said he wanted to. She was busy rolling up the sleeves of one of Albert's shirts that she liked to sleep in, her thin legs sticking out like two pins. Jacob put his hand on her back to guide her into bed. His large hand spanned wider than her scapula that stuck out and formed two smooth hills. She was almost eleven and particularly smart-aleck, but Jacob wondered if she had reason to be.

"So, listen," Jacob pulled the covers around her. "I told Ty I'd take the two of you to the circus. Not tomorrow, but next Friday." Cedar said she would go, but that she was getting pretty tired of circuses. Jacob searched her face for a flicker of joy, and thought he caught one.

"You gonna stay long?" Cedar asked. The lines of her face went back further in time than Ty's. Her large eyes reflected a blue that Jacob remembered in his father's grandmother, an immigrant woman who came from Germany to Tennessee and had in some way endowed this young girl with a fierce pride that had not had time to soften. Propped on her pillow in Albert's shirt, she had a look of hollowed-out stone, as if someone had shouted at her and the shout had echoed.

"I'll be here about two weeks," Jacob told her. He sat on the bed to see if they could think of anything else to say.

"Maybe you could visit me in Virginia." Cedar smiled, her large eyes rising. "Ty could come too," Jacob said.

"Mama wouldn't let both of us."

"Well, maybe just you." And it seemed to be what she wanted to hear.

Jacob had two sons, even now considered he had two sons, though Joseph died at age twelve. When people asked, Jacob said he had two sons, but after a moment would say one had died in childhood with a disease passed down through the generations on his father's side. And though the disease had lain quiet inside the body of Jacob himself and inside the body of his father, it had flared in Joseph.

Joseph grew sick in November with a bad cold but by early spring was dead. Jacob and Molly watched and as Joseph became sicker, they wanted to say something, call him back.

But on the last day they knew, and the other son, Tom, said, "We ought to go outside now." He spoke several times before his parents heard, saying, "We ought to go outside now." It was a beautiful day, the warmth of summer beginning that day. Tom was seven and he ran ahead of his parents, knowing they would watch him. He jumped at frogs, bringing one back to show them. And every now and then he told them to hurry or come on, and their steps might quicken, hasten maybe toward the promise that came with the season and with this son who led them across the field as though they were on a lead line, as though he were bringing easy-to-handle cows home after a day in a different pasture. But the sunlight was warm, and to anyone else this day held a perfect air.

The funeral was the next day and as Jacob held Tom in his lap, he wondered how he would live tomorrow. Molly sat beside him, her arm hooked through Jacob's arm. Halfway through the service she took Tom from Jacob's lap, holding the boy close to her, but not wanting Tom really, wanting

Joseph instead, which made nobody feel very good. So she put Tom between the two of them, all of them sitting as separate as stones. When the service was over, and the graveside part was over, Molly asked if they would like to do something before going home. Tom asked "What?" and Jacob could not imagine what Molly would suggest.

"We could get some ice cream," she said, as if they had been on an outing and would end it this way.

"Okay," said Jacob, going along.

So they stopped at the Ice Cream Parlor, which is still called that same name. They sat in a booth and ordered in their Sunday clothes, though it was Tuesday. It would be three years before Molly could enter that parlor again, but Jacob took Tom whenever he wanted.

Tom now was thirty-five, and lived on a hillside in Vermont where the mountains and hills looked much the same as the hills in Virginia or Tennessee. He was a lawyer and came to Virginia two or three times a year, usually bringing his two children and his wife. He would come this year for Christmas.

Jacob unpacked the rest of his clothes and hung them on the wooden hangers Annie had left for him. He noticed the curtains starched crisp as paper and appreciated Annie's attentions toward him. But the memory-force of Verna standing in the kitchen with the new Joseph's head propped by her hair entered him like an ache. And he tried to remember why he had come back here.

Yesterday, while waiting at the train station for Annie to pick him up, someone saw Jacob, called to him, said "You here to hunt, Jake?" Jacob carried his long rifle in a leather case and draped over his arm were two hunting coats, and a vest.

"No." Then "Well, yes," Jacob said, "but that's not why I came back," and he proceeded to go through reasons with the stranger (or the man who recognized him, but whom he did not recognize). And there was a woman standing beside the man. They both nodded and understood that Jacob had not come back for hunting, but for something else. "You see," Jacob explained, or thought he needed to explain, as though he had been caught doing something, or neglecting to do something, "I came to see Callie again." His voice trailed off as he looked around for Annie's face in the crowd.

"Are you still teaching?" the woman asked. They knew all about Jacob.

"History, some literature," Jacob told her, thinking she probably knew already. "But I took some time off." He wished Annie would hurry. He pointed to his gun and began to explain why he brought it, so that the man and the woman were both confused as to whether or not he was saying that he really had come to hunt or if he meant that there was another more important reason he was there.

Then Jacob said how tired he was and the woman mentioned that she hoped he had slept on the train. When Annie walked up and greeted the two people by saying their names, she hugged Jacob, then nodded to the couple in a way that indicated dismissal. They watched the couple amble off.

"What were you telling them?" Annie asked. "They looked confused, as if they weren't sure they were talking to the right person."

"They weren't." Jacob laughed, then said, "They asked why I was here. I was having a hard time telling them."

"For a visit." Annie said. "Tell them you came for a visit."

Jacob guessed she was right, and it seemed all his life that what he expected to be simple or easy had never turned out to be so, and those things that appeared complicated usually had an obvious solution.

"Where did you park the car?" he asked. He picked up the luggage and gave one piece to Annie to carry.

Annie draped some of his heavy coats over her arm and carried the one small bag Jacob gave to her. She looked around trying to remember where she had parked her car in the new parking lot, which was not large, but even so the city council had decided to put signs with animal pictures to help people remember their location. The animals confused her.

"Is this a trick question?" she asked.

Failure to Eat Bread

The telephone rang. It was late and Jacob imagined it was Molly. He was right.

"Telephone, Jake," Annie yelled from downstairs.

Molly said that Tom had called and wanted to come hunt for a few days.

"Why?" Jacob asked. He wasn't pleased, didn't want Tom or anybody with him this visit.

"He just wants to, Jake," Molly said.

"He doesn't even *like* to hunt."

"Oh, Jake. Let him do it."

Jacob knew that Tom tried to be both sons to him, though it had never been necessary. Jacob knew, too, that he had tried to do the same thing with his own father and thought that that probably wasn't necessary either. He thought of his father and his sons, his mind moving back and forth as if a long chord had been struck, one that lingered, longed to be struck again.

"Well, anyway," Molly said. "How *is* everything? Seen Callie yet?"

"No." Jacob's answer was curt, so Molly decided to just tell him good night and that she'd talk to him in a few days. "Okay," Jacob said, then "Here. You want to talk to Annie?" He handed the phone to his sister.

* * *

Molly loved Jacob so much that when he was gone from her she would bring his face to her mind and her heart ached with his absence, even after all these years of marriage that sweet ache came back. She had told him on the phone, just now, how she missed him. Though Jacob didn't reciprocate. As he went down the hallway to his room, he wished he had said something nice to her. Their marriage was good—a rare thing these days. But all their years had not been good ones.

There were years in the middle of their married life when Jacob and Molly no longer loved each other, or thought they didn't, or at least no longer felt the way they felt when they met. It was about the time Joseph got sick with what started out as a cold. And though they never expected to lose him so quickly, or at all, something filled them with a sense of dread. So they put this on each other. Quarreling. Molly wanted to teach school. Jacob said she shouldn't. They were both unhappy during that time and regretted now that this last time with Joseph had been so quarrelsome. But they admitted that Joseph probably didn't notice.

Molly came to Jacob's mind—how she had been then, and earlier, how she had been. And Jacob thought how in those first days of being in love, he wanted to be with the one he loved, observing an independence and charm that attracted him. Then he found that the same charm later became cause for distance and gave them trouble in marriage, made them feel alone. Those qualities which were first loved because they were not his were later scorned for the same reason, until eventually the qualities became his own and the love enlarged. And it was something different, better than he imagined in those early romantic days.

There was nothing special about the way they had met.

He passed her at the county fair as he walked with a friend and she with several girls. The day was humid and her hair frizzed, giving her face a fullness it did not really possess. Her long oval face seemed almost severe if not for the wideness of her mouth. And though Jacob looked at her with the casualness of one who expects to nod, it was with all his senses, leaning slightly toward her.

She had not broken her stride while passing him, her walk giving the impression of aloofness. But the look she cut toward him held a different promise, so Jacob felt proud to see past the vulnerability that lay at her mouth and the edges of her hair. And though it was not exactly a meeting, that was the way they first met and how they remembered it.

During the next week Jacob saw her twice. The first time he asked her name. The second time he asked her to go with him to the fair. He suffered in his effort to ask, trying to think of ways to appear nonchalant. When he did blurt out an invitation and she said Yes, he was not prepared, so she said Yes again and he said Fine, then told her what time he would pick her up.

She wore a yellow dress and sandals. It was the beginning of summer. As she climbed into the front seat of the car, she let her hands finger the soft yellow cotton, rubbing it all the way to the hem. She was eighteen and Jacob was almost twenty.

They ate dinner at a concession stand run by The Church of the Good Shepherd, which was known for having the best barbecue and coleslaw, but their desserts were dry looking cakes with sauce running down the sides, so they went to have dessert with First Baptist whose barbecue, people said, tasted like cardboard, but whose cakes would melt in your mouth. After that, they rode several rides, ending with the Ferris wheel.

They looked up to the highest chair and Jacob asked Molly if she wanted to ride. Molly nodded. The seat of the Ferris wheel whisked down to a wooden platform and the man operating the ride opened the iron bar and closed it around them with a cell-door sound that made them both jump. She took hold of his hand.

As they ascended, the wind blew Molly's hair around her face. She let go of the iron bar, and Jacob's hand, and, breathing in, let her arms float upward. When Jacob looked at her, he wondered if she might be afraid of falling; but her face held no fear. She had her arms in the air as high as she could reach. And as they rode over the side, Jacob could hear her make a noise, a hum that came from some place low and lasted long, one that seemed to burst from her all at once each time they crested the top and would last like a long breath all the way down. And she made that sound each time, so that Jacob looked forward to it.

From the top he could see the view of the Tennessee River, the lights of stores in town, and one long barge loaded with coal moving its searchlight from bank to bank. They went around and around as Molly reached with her arms and the wind blew the good smell of her hair. The deep low hum and the white arms reaching high and long, affecting Jacobs as nothing ever had. And when they stopped and the man unlocked the iron bar, Jacob was afraid he wanted to marry her.

For many days in a row they saw each other, visiting parks to sit on a bench and share popcorn with the birds. They watched children playing on the swings and seesaw. Sometimes they watched without speaking as might someone who stands before a painting that he has heard about or seen pictures of, but has never experienced. And the experience is one of being absorbed into the painting itself, becoming lost for a moment inside the scene until he hears others walking behind him. But when he leaves, part of it goes with him. And sometimes they pretended the children were their own so that when they got up to leave felt their life was full and more joyous than it really was.

Jacob would touch her hand or her waist as he directed her

41

through the door. He would lay his fingertips on her waist, resting them for a moment as she walked. And he felt a strong fiber of muscle moving beneath her dress, her hips rising slightly with each step. He wanted to keep his hand there and wondered if she would like him to, but she turned her head when they walked through the doorway as if to tell him That was enough. And he knew he must go slow with this girl, because what she had in mind would take a whole lifetime and he wasn't sure he wanted to give that much, so he waited. But when she turned to look at him and he had not said anything to make her turn, she held his eyes as surely as if she had him by the shoulders. And he thought at that time that one lifetime would not be enough and wanted to blurt out his feelings, but instead asked if she was chilly, because she was shivering and he could see the thin whiteness of her arms emerging from her short-sleeved dress. And he was amazed at her frailty.

On their wedding night they sat on the edge of their bed. Molly looked as though she might bolt at any moment. Jacob tried to ease her. And though at first she did not sit close beside him, she leaned to make up for it. But finally she moved closer. As they talked, Jacob slipped his arm to her waist, squeezing her, but making his movements quick to emphasize a point. Then he moved his whole body to kiss her cheek in mid-sentence, not to emphasize anything, but as though he couldn't help it.

She found it difficult to listen or to make sense of what he said or to answer in a controlled way, so she stood up. Jacob thought she might leave, but she went to the other room. When she came back, Jacob found that she did not have the frailty he expected, nor did she have the shyness. Her body exuded strong health.

It was not the moment Jacob wanted to think of Alma's Truck Stop, but he did. He was sixteen, and a woman (presumably Alma) began to talk to him, wiping the counter and asking more from him than payment for pie and coffee.

As Jacob looked at Alma's mouth, he had a moment's fright, because her mouth seemed suddenly huge with words pouring out at him as if she were shouting, and he thought maybe she was. He didn't listen, but nodded appropriately. She told him this summer had been the worst and how the fan had broke. Her face loomed so close that Jacob felt the need to stare at the floor or to search for something far off to rivet his mind to.

She stopped talking and when he looked up, her round fat face saw the revulsion he felt for her. And he was sorry. He put his hand on her shoulder, nodding to whatever she had told him.

She wiped the counter for the fiftieth time.

Jacob looked on her pocket at the red stitching that spelled Alma in longhand and Alma picked at the small piece of crust left on his plate. She popped it into her mouth.

Her husband had run off three months ago, she told Jacob, and she chewed the crust slowly. "I won't marry no more." She wanted him to understand what she needed. "Anyway," but she didn't finish her statement and Jacob could only guess.

The place was empty now, the lunch crowd gone back to work, and Alma led Jacob to the room behind the kitchen.

"I want you to know," Jacob said. But Alma's smile interrupted him. She shook her head.

Alma was in her early thirties, almost twice as old as Jacob, though she looked even older. As she undressed, he noticed that she was not as fat all over as she was in the face. She had a beauty that at the moment neither attracted nor repelled him, but left him indifferent. She was exactly the kind of woman he wanted to have the first time: someone he would not owe anything to, someone who would not expect him to call the next day, who might not even remember what he looked like. This anonymity gave him a chance to learn his finesse. Because being the young man that he was, he thought he could learn what a woman likes and when the real thing came along he could apply what he knew and appear experienced and worldly.

But Molly was the one who appeared experienced, worldly. For she approached Jacob with the movements of a large cat, her attack slow and easy. And Jacob could feel her all over him as if she were two people. When she was finished, she reached up high and long as though she were falling, and Jacob could hear the hum he expected to hear. And when they came down, he felt a cool breeze blowing across their bed, hearing the music of the county fair in his head, and the Ferris wheel where he first knew he would marry her.

But the children grew older and their life changed. And that change seemed to be clear to Jacob one night while they sat on their porch. It was June and the air smelled like melons. But Jacob felt saddened, a quick sadness that flowed over him and through him and left him soaked with a kind of heaviness that was difficult to ignore. He sat with Molly on the porch, and though she had said nothing to sadden him, he felt the presence of something changed.

"Tomorrow," he said, telling Molly something he had probably already told her, but wanting to break the voluminous silence. "Tomorrow," and he got up to get his piece of bread that he had each night. Going to the kitchen to get bread with butter, spreading the butter to every edge. It was a ritual he enjoyed nightly for so many years. But as he started to rise, pushing up with his arms, Molly turned and took hold of his forearm with a grip like a vise and said, "I can't stand it." And she said it so low and quiet that Jacob thought he had misunderstood, thought she had said something about the weather or the children's colds. Then she said it again at the same level tone and when Jacob looked at her he knew indeed she couldn't stand it, but he didn't know what it was that she was unable to bear. And he hoped it wasn't himself. "What?" He covered her hand with his own. "What is it?" But Molly pulled away. "Jake," she said, "it's not the way I imagined."

Jacob did not know what Molly had imagined, but found that he resented her. He didn't want to resent her, because she seemed to need his help, but instead of helping he withdrew and said nothing. So they sat together that night on the porch, beside each other but as separate as they had ever been. And he wondered if Molly wished she had never said it, because something now would not be the same. Jacob would begin to wonder if she was unhappy, whereas before he had never wondered or even thought about it. And it was as if she had never been unhappy until that night, so Jacob took it as a criticism of himself. He hoped she was sorry and even thought that her misery now was deserved, a just punishment for spoiling his night.

He turned to see if she might take it back, or say she was in a mood and that it would pass. If she had said that, he would be willing to let it go, forget it. But her face looked like stone and Jacob suddenly realized that there was a whole side of this woman he did not know, and that maybe, he did not even like. And he stared at her as though she had just come in and sat down and should introduce herself.

"Molly?" he said, to make sure this was she.

"Hmmm?" and her voice hummed a sweet remembrance through his bones. She turned to face him, her eyes bold as a bird's. And though Jacob felt her separation and resented her for this wedge, he loved her, whoever she was.

"It's time to go in," he told her.

But they sat for a few more minutes, deciding again to stay. Not leaving each other as they sometimes wanted to, but staying, wishing they had the strength to walk away, imagining they did. But staying, because the need for each other was stronger than the need to walk away.

When they stood up to go inside, Molly asked if he forgot to eat his bread and offered to get it for him. When Jacob didn't answer, she said, "You forgot to eat your bread." He had. He said he had. But he told her there were other things he had not forgotten in all these years.

Jacob undressed and slipped beneath the sheets of the fourposter. As he turned out the light, moonlight moved into the room, blending everything together, the furniture, the walls, and even Jacob lying there becoming part of the room. The pale soft light brushed over everything as if it were sleep itself. And Jacob knew that if sleep could be seen it would look like this, melting around him. But when morning came and everything rose together with the sun, his eyes would open, and even the furniture would lift slightly and loosen itself from sleep.

Jacob could hear Annie still speaking softly on the phone. What were they talking about? He had closed the door, closing himself off in much the same way his father had done. He thought of his father closed in a room for so many years, drinking. Jacob closed himself off too, only he didn't use drink—had promised himself never to need it. Still, he thought with some surprise, he had done something similar.

It was a late afternoon in 1945 when Jacob went to see his father. Jacob had returned from the war and arrived to find Karl in the bedroom, his door closed. Karl had been drinking for many years by then and in fact Jacob's mother wrote to Jacob to prepare him for the condition in which he might find his father when he returned.

Jacob knocked and heard a sound he assumed meant to come in. The light entered the room from the tall windows, coming in in dark yellow slants and was such that his father couldn't see Jacob standing in the doorway. He was in a kind of stupor, but he turned, hearing something, though not seeing anything. He turned back to his bottle beside the bed, another lying empty on the floor.

Jacob spoke again. Karl said What? too loudly, as if the act of both seeing and hearing was more than he could accomplish, and he would need to choose which he would do. Then his father grew suddenly affectionate, maudlin even, standing to throw himself toward Jacob, stumbling, catching himself, apologizing. He cried a bit. Then he gathered himself together, putting the bottle down on the table in a way that indicated he had finished, maybe finished even with this whole business of drinking all day. He motioned for Jacob to sit on the bed.

"Are you all right?" he asked. He had asked this twice already and both times Jacob said Fine. Fine. But he asked again.

"Yes." They spoke for a while. Jacob wondered if his father knew the war was over.

"Is it over?" he asked as if reading Jacob's mind. He had been staring at the pocket of Jacob's uniform.

"Yes."

"And you're all right?" But this time he took hold of Jacob's arm, testing.

Karl had begun lately to quote passages from *Psalms*— not correctly or precisely, but saying parts of it in the old language as he remembered it. He kept saying one portion over and over. He would stand and make himself a drunken psalmist: "I am so sad," he would pronounce, "that I forgot to eat my bread." Jacob could not help but laugh when he said it, not at what he said, but at the histrionics.

When Jacob left his father's room, he had been there for two hours. Much of the time was spent waiting for his father to respond to something or hearing him pronounce his sadness and failure to eat bread. His mother was in the hallway. The way she lifted her hand toward him was like a stranger.

"How do you think he is?" she asked.

"Not as bad as I thought," Jacob lied. He was so much worse.

"Well, good." His mother believed. Her hair was disheveled and her eyes seemed not so large. She looked to Jacob like a woman he had seen only a few times before.

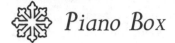 *Piano Box*

A piano box had been left beside the road next to Garr's woods. It couldn't be seen from the road, and was far enough into the woods that it might be mistaken for a toolshed or a pumphouse.

Jacob saw it when Cedar pointed it out. "See that?" Cedar said.

"What?"

"It's a piano box," Ty's voice. He and Cedar had already seen it up close, played in it. Jacob was bringing them home from school. "Wanna see it?"

Jacob squinted and thought he saw a shedlike thing in the woods, but wasn't sure. He didn't want to stop and see it.

"Sure," he said.

Both children lifted slightly in their seats. Jacob pulled the car over onto the road's shoulder.

"How do you know it's a piano box?" Jacob asked, getting out. The children ran ahead of him. Cedar pointed to the label on the side that said Baldwin Piano Makers, and another—This End Up. Jacob decided it was proof enough and asked whose piano they thought came in it.

The box was big enough for Ty to stand upright. Cedar had to bend only slightly to get in, but could stand upright when she stood inside. Jacob leaned down to get in and when he stood inside, only his neck and head had to curve downward. He looked like a tall sunflower. They all sat down.

"I've only been inside twice," said Cedar. "I think the piano went to Miss Hatley. She's the music teacher and her old piano was awful. Out of tune and everything. So the church bought her one to give lessons on, but she has to keep it at the church, in one of the Sunday-school rooms." Cedar stood and walked around. One board was cracked and hung loose, so she tore it off and looked out of the space she had created, using it as a window. Ty talked to Jacob.

"You think it would be warm enough?"

"For what?"

"To sleep in. I'd like to sleep in here."

"By yourself?" Cedar asked. She couldn't believe it.

"No." He looked to Jacob. "With somebody."

"Not me." said Cedar, then she thought and said, "Mama wouldn't let us."

They both looked to Jacob. "Oh, I don't know." He was having to do so many things he didn't want to do. "We'll ask her," he said.

That night Verna said she didn't see any sense in it, but that if they wanted to stay all night out there in the piano box, they'd better do it before it got any colder.

They decided on Tuesday night, because Wednesday was a teacher's workday and Cedar and Ty didn't have to go to school.

"Tuesday then," Jacob said and hoped to some extent that they might decide against it by then. "If you still want to." Their faces showed no promise that they might change their minds.

Tuesday night Verna gave the children a hearty, hot meal and wrapped them in clothes that would keep them properly warm. She gave Jacob enough blankets and sleeping bags to make three comfortable pallets to sleep on.

"We're fixed up," said Jacob and found that he was now looking forward to the outing and glad they had not decided against it. Cedar brought two candles and her radio, Ty brought a deck of cards, a large heavy-duty flashlight, and his Indian knife in its sheath. Jacob did not bring anything, but carried all the bedding to seem as if he had. Then Verna handed them a sack of apples, some cookies, raisins, and a thermos of hot cocoa.

"What'll you do about breakfast in the morning?" Verna asked.

Jacob said they would stop and eat at Sophie's and Ned's on the way back. Verna thought that was fine. Her baby was asleep on her shoulder, so she put him down and hugged them all good-bye. When she hugged Jacob, he thought how she smelled of soured milk.

It was already dark when they settled themselves into the piano box. Jacob propped the flashlight in the window Cedar had made, so they could see the place to lay out their beds.

When they were settled, Cedar suggested Ty get the cards and she lit the candles.

"What'll we play?" Jacob asked.

Cedar mentioned a new game she had learned and wanted to teach it to them. She announced it and dealt six cards to each person. She told them the rules and assured them it was easy.

They played for nearly an hour, Jacob still not catching on completely, and accusing Cedar of changing the rules as soon as he thought he had learned everything. When he suggested that they quit, he received no arguments, and Ty blew out the candles, but the flashlight was still on and gave the box the look of a room with an overhead light.

"Leave that on," said Cedar.

They climbed into their sleeping bags and Jacob lifted the covers to get under them. "It's cold," he said, and hoped they might huddle close together to stay warm. No one suggested it.

51

Jacob thought they might talk, but the only sound was the low sound of Cedar's radio and the crickets left over from summer. Not many crickets sounded now, so that their sound was as low and quiet as the radio and seemed a little like static. It was not long before Jacob heard the slow steady breathing of children asleep. He turned off the flashlight and drifted into a doze himself, though not expecting to sleep well or comfortably he was surprised at how comfortable and warm he felt. Jacob dreamed. He dreamed he was running, but as he dreamed he thought he was running toward something, and that he would soon be there. He was in the woods, but not a woods he had ever seen before. Sometimes in the dream he thought people were chasing him, so he couldn't tell if he were running toward something or away. He remembered only his stumbling, and a frustration within the dream that kept tripping him, a slow motion kind of falling that comes in dreams when the arms flail out and the falling is one of complete falling, with an inability to catch yourself or break the fall. So he stumbled, hitting the ground (which he had never before done in a dream), but then there was the getting up that came even slower, and with more struggle. When he was finally up, he knew that he felt older and that maybe the whole process had taken many years, so that he was not the same person he was when the falling began.

He woke to Ty calling out. Ty was talking in his sleep. The night was almost over and the light that came through Cedar's torn-out window was the deep dim light of earliest morning. Ty called out louder. Cedar woke.

"What's he saying?" Jacob asked. He couldn't tell.

"That's our daddy's name," said Cedar. "Sometimes he calls out daddy's name."

"What is it? What's he saying?"

Then they heard it again. Ty's voice struck a low chord, his voice groggy. "Edward," he called out—a two note rhythmic interruption given in a mechanical meter, then repeated, contrasting slightly and beginning on a different note. He called the name three times.

"That's what he calls him?" asked Jacob.

"He doesn't even know him really. Doesn't remember him like I do. But Mother calls him that. She says 'Edward says this' and 'Edward says that.' And I don't know if he ever really says anything, about us I mean, but Mother tells us he does and tries to make us feel good."

"What do *you* remember?"

It already seemed like morning. The light changing and entering the piano box in more places than Cedar's window. The whole room-box had a light now so Jacob could see that Cedar was propped on her elbows, Ty lying flat. He called *Edward* again.

"Does he say anything else, or just that? That name."

"Sometimes. He asks for things in his sleep."

Cedar's voice contrasted to Ty's, who called out in two notes. Cedar's voice resonated clear and had chords that if they were sung would have carried the full weight of a tune. And Jacob wondered what his own voice carried, here in this box that had held Miss Hatley's piano.

"I remember one thing," said Cedar, going back to answer Jacob's question. "I remember he carried me on his back when he put me to bed at night. That was when I was about three."

"Did he ever carry Ty?"

Cedar looked at Ty. No. They could both see Ty's face and chest uncovered. His shirt, that he had slept in unbuttoned, was open in a way that seemed embarrassingly revealing. But he did not call out anymore, and when they woke up for good, after dozing until the light came all the way in, filling the box with thin rays that came through the slits, Jacob suggested they go to Sophie's for breakfast. And after taking everything to the car, Jacob asked Ty to jump on his back and he'd carry him that way. Cedar walked along beside them, without commenting.

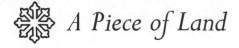 *A Piece of Land*

It was a diner, but everyone called it Sophie's and Ned's. There was always at least one fly on the countertop, others buzzing around the sugar jars. Baskets of hard bread were left out for customers and years of indulgence kept people coming back. Soldier, still retarded and living longer than anyone thought he would, was seated at the counter telling Sophie jokes. Sophie looked annoyed, but when she saw Jacob she brightened and lifted a plate toward him in greeting.

As Jacob and the children entered the diner, a fat, yellow bar of sunlight fell across the floor and up one wall as if it were a ribbon thrown down to announce their arrival. Tables lined the walls or sat in the middle of the room. Ned worked at the grill, but Jacob could see him through the window that divided the main room from the kitchen. He set down dishes of food for Sophie to hand out. She served at the counter that seated six comfortably, eight uncomfortably.

Sophie called for Jake to sit at the table nearest the counter, then turned to the kitchen. "Ned, give Jake those eggs with cheese. He'll like that," and she went over to ask the children what they wanted. Jacob shook hands with Ned through the serving window—a greasy, vigorous pump.

Ned asked Jake if he was going hunting, though as he asked he expected Jacob to go. "Jake, that land is still the wildest I've ever seen." Ned slapped four sausages onto the grill and scrambled a pile of eggs with cheese. "Why, Ed Holcomb saw an animal up there two weeks ago, said he didn't even know what it *was*."

One wave of people left, another came in. Sophic took orders then brought two cups of coffee to the table. She asked Soldier to hand out food from Ned's window. Soldier was glad to. He had done that before.

Sophie was short and had dyed black hair. Her hair had always been dark, but now was impudent and dull and imparted to her a rigidity that she had probably earned. She was the kind of person whose malice was not yet conscious, but would be in ten years maybe. In years, she would learn to say things calculated to hurt people, and this quality would develop in her for two reasons. One, she had no children and felt she had to pretend she didn't mind, and two, she could not experience the intensity she wanted from people's caring so she sought it in their anger. And as she grew older she realized that her need for passion was finally more important than the people around her.

But she had a tender side. For at times she appeared childlike so that her lips would swell and her face and cheeks seemed to rise up like a mask put on from the chin rather than over the head. Her face grew soft now as she sat next to the children, not saying anything for a few moments, just sitting and putting salt on her egg.

"I sometimes come here early in the morning," she told Jacob, confiding something that Jacob did not have all the parts of. "I come here and sit." Her voice spoke pieces of what she had already told him in her mind.

Jacob remembered Sophie as a girl, young, though he couldn't picture her young anymore. She was in her early forties, but her hard-face make-up and her beauty-parlor-curly hair were bent toward making her young, though instead it left hardly a trace of youthfulness.

"And I sit," she confided to the children now, though they

55

didn't listen, had not said anything since they came in.

"Late at night?" Jacob asked, wanting to say something. He half-listened, half-looked around for someone familiar.

"Early." Sophie had quick, short answers, giving an economy in her speech that seemed to indicate ill-temper. Jacob nodded and kept eating.

Sophie pointed to the booth where she would sit. Four men sat crowded into the booth now and Jacob pictured Sophie sitting in it herself in the early mornings. "I keep it dark, you know." Jacob knew. "I keep the light off so that I can sit and watch the light creep in, see it fill up this room by seven o'clock." She held up her hands as though she were giving benediction. Jacob didn't know how to respond.

Usually, Sophie talked about children so that the listener would realize she was glad she did not have any, but today she seemed to be telling Jacob how she mourned them in the early morning as she sat in the booth. At least that was the way Jacob understood her. As she talked, her features loosened, like a baby's, and even her hair plastered and sprayed to an unnatural height and texture, eased itself around her face.

"We slept in the piano box," Ty told her, proud and with the spirit of a braggart.

"What's that?" Sophie asked.

"That's the box that Miss Hatley's piano came in," Cedar told her.

Sophie screwed up her face to show distaste for Miss Hatley, who had never set foot inside Sophie's and Ned's and never would.

"We stayed in it all night," Ty's plate was empty. He had eaten his eggs and toast so quickly. Jacob asked if he wanted a doughnut or something. He said he did, so Sophie got up to get the doughnut plate for him.

"That might be fun," Sophie said in response to the piano box, but she probably didn't mean it.

56

"You can go with us next time," Ty said and took two doughnuts. Sophie smiled, then clapped her hands and changed the subject.

"You came back to see Callie?" Sophie asked Jacob, but it was more of a statement. Jacob wondered how Sophie knew.

"Yes," he said, without any certainty if that were true.

"She's about to die," said Sophie and wiped her mouth with the primness of a very rich lady. "I went by to see her yesterday. She doesn't get many visitors. Nobody really. I took her some food." She paused and laid down her fork. She leaned toward Jacob, "Because," she holler-whispered, "I don't want it known that that woman starved to death down there, and me and Ned here with all this food." She waved her arms as though she were showing a row of banquet tables. Jacob nodded. Sophie turned to see Soldier balancing four plates on his hands and arms. "Yesterday I went. She said something about you. Asked if you were here. I told her I hadn't seen you, but that you were here."

"It's been a long time," said Jacob, "but Annie and Albert, they tell me about her when I call." Jacob had not seen Callie for seven years. As a boy, though, he had seen her almost every day.

Whenever Callie met Jacob on the street or in his house, she felt the bones in his shoulders and back as if she were making a diagnosis. She was tall, a lean woman with short straight hair cut close to a pretty face. She didn't have children of her own, but treated Jacob as if he were hers. Jacob grew to expect her firm, hard grip against his back and shoulder blades. And as Callie grew older, her hands turned thin and birdlike and felt as warm as a hot poultice to his skin. Jacob felt a healing power in her gestures and thought she might be magical.

But something happened to Callie. And though Jacob was too young to remember it, he remembered hearing the story through the years, how it was whispered and told

57

in parlors. And Callie wore that story as surely as a shawl.

She had stopped one night to help a boy standing on the road. She had been married one year. Everyone already thought of her as an old maid. She taught school, fifth grade. But then she married Ruben Locke, who owned Locke's Grocery Store.

She saw the boy leaning down as if he might be hurt or something, so she pulled off the road to see what was wrong. When he stood up, she saw his face and still thought he was just a boy, though it was hard to tell. He looked both old and young, and had an innocence about him, Callie said. Though his skin was coarse and rough and didn't tell lies.

Callie asked if she could help and the boy came around to her car door. With one jerk he opened it and yanked Callie across the field to a small outhouse near Garr's woods. He talked incoherently, Callie told, calling her Faye somebody. And she kept wondering whether or not the car door was closed.

Her legs were scratched from stickers and low branches, so she tried to rub them. The boy, who did not look like a boy, was large and found it easy to push Callie through the door of the outhouse. It hung by the top hinge, and he didn't even bother to pull it shut. It was not yet dark.

Callie said she screamed or thought she had screamed, not hearing the sound at first, but feeling a fullness in her throat that had risen of its own accord and could not be held back or down. And she knew it must have come out in a scream, because he kept telling her to shut up. But later she remembered she had vomited.

He took both her arms and shook her, telling her to stop that noise, and then she heard it, a high-pitched, odd sound that seemed as though it were coming from somewhere inside herself. The boy spit a brown stream and it hit the wall of the shed. She watched it slide down the boards as he said,

"I'm not going to hurt you. You think I'm going to hurt you?"
And Callie wondered what he would have done if he meant to
hurt her.

When she looked at him again, she looked straight at his
face and she could see through the glass of her own anxious
mind that he was not as old as she, but older than he looked.
She saw that he would never be free or feel the peace he must
have thought he should feel, or thought he should have come
to by this age. She tried to imagine him beyond the glass frame,
but couldn't.

He pushed with his own body against her, pinning her to
the wall. Her legs were trapped between the toilet and the
corner board. With one hand he unbuckled his overalls, the
other hand leaned into the corner. Callie said he looked up at
the ceiling where there was a hole and the last of the day's
light. And for a moment they both saw a bird fly across the
space of that hole, then she said he looked around to the sides
as if he were studying how to build a shed like this for himself.
She hoped he would change his mind, but his clothes dropped
to the ground, and at this point in telling the story, whoever
was telling would make sure the listener knew that he was
completely naked, and that this was the kind of man who wore
no underwear, as if this alone were as unforgivable as anything that was to follow.

The toilet was stained brown, was filled with water but had
not been cleaned in years. The smell made her feel sick and
she wondered if she were getting the flu. He quickly tore her
underpants, and in their struggle some of the water over-
flowed from a place that was leaking below the bowl. It rushed
over their ankles.

Callie remembered hearing him leave. She saw him pick up
a leaf to wipe himself. Then she sank to the ground, not caring
where she sat or how dirty she might be, because she would
never be as dirty as she was right then. She sat until someone

found her car on the road and called to her, finally walking to the shed and turning a flashlight to her face. It was Mr. Garr. He asked what was the matter and told her she had left the car door open, and he hoped the battery hadn't burned down. Callie said she had the flu. Mr. Garr lifted her carefully and took her to the doctor.

There was another story too, about how that traveling boy disappeared. Jacob never knew the details, only that his daddy and Ruben Locke left the next day and came home late. Sarah waited up. The sheriff came out saying they never found that boy and what a shame that was, but that he'd probably never be out this way again anyhow.

But Jacob heard another tale of that boy, how he had been tied to a tree next to Garr's woods and chopped up with an ax so that there wasn't even any need to cut him down, because pieces of him lay all around the tree. And one time Jacob's good friend Phillip (who was from the richest family in town and liked Jacob because Phillip liked to have at least one middle-class friend) took Jacob to that tree and showed him the dark heavy blot.

Jacob wondered as the tree grew taller if the stain would get higher and higher until it was at eye level, or so high that nobody would think of it anymore. But Phillip said it would take a long time, and Jacob said he would never forget it, no matter how high that tree grew.

Jacob pictured Callie in the same place where she lived all those years with Ruben Locke over Locke's Store. Ruben had been dead for twenty years now. "Is she still over the store?"

When Sophie shook her head no, Jacob must have looked either surprised or disappointed, because Sophie quickly said, "She moved out near the cave. She *wanted* to. She asked me and Ned to take her out there. We helped her fix it up. Lord knows why she wanted to be so far out. Must be a mile and

a half, which isn't so bad except that sometimes she *walks* it."
Sophie touched again the corners of her mouth. "But we still
take care of her." She patted Jacob's hand in a way both con-
soling and dismissing, then she smiled a smile that wasn't
real, but made her eyes squint. She added, "Annie goes out
there sometimes, and Mr. Brown does. They take her
groceries."

Soldier handed out plates, making mistakes but mostly
getting it right. Sophie told him he was doing good, and he
beamed. Soldier was fifty-three years old this year. "And
Soldier goes out every now and then," said Sophie, "at least
I've seen him come back from there, though I've never seen
him actually *there*."

Something made Jacob angry: either Sophie talking about
Callie as an outsider or else maybe thinking of Callie alone
out in the woods living in a dilapidated house he remembered
from boyhood. "But you," he said, then changed it to "This
town has *always*," but he couldn't think of a word accusing
enough so he stopped and the omission was more accusing
than anything he could have thought of.

Sophie bristled. "Well, Jake." Her face and hair regained
their solidity. "Let's talk for a minute about what *you* ever did
for her." And she said it the way women can say things like
that when they have spent their lives taking care of and doing
for people what you yourself only worry about. "When I saw
her, her voice was raspy," Sophie said after a brief silence,
"like she hadn't talked with anyone for a while."

Sophie went back to work. Jacob sat a while longer, drank
coffee that Soldier was directed to bring him. The children
grew restless and begged to leave, telling Jacob they would
walk home along the railroad track and how they did it all the
time. Jacob allowed them to leave, and didn't find out until
later that they had never walked home along the railroad
tracks.

"Hello, Soldier," Jacob said, as Soldier filled his coffee cup. He didn't know if Soldier remembered him. Soldier nodded, without smiling. His face looked startled, as if Jacob had spoken too loudly. His face, Jacob thought, looked like an empty room with its closet doors thrown wide open.

It was almost eleven and the sun no longer hit the walls but came in across the tables, shined on the sugar jars and scattered the rays the way the sun shines on posts of a brass bed. As Jacob left the diner, he noticed Soldier had left a little before him and stood looking into a store window. He appeared to be reading something, his expression so intent that for a moment he resembled a pale statue of great intelligence. Jacob hadn't seen or even thought of him in so many years. The town didn't call him Soldier until Jacob had gone away. Jacob knew him as Oliver. As he looked at Oliver now, he could see even from across the street, a slackness that people don't usually show in their face, a relaxed tension of a kind that deadens the face more than sleep. Because in sleep there is repose, but this slackening of vitality gave the air around Oliver a complacency, and the careless quality of his eyes were enhanced as he lifted his head and the symmetry of his nose and chin and forehead were evident.

Jacob walked until he came to a grove of tall willows. Callie had shown him this grove when he was a boy, and standing in it, it still had the effect of a cathedral. Maybe more so now. But he wished he were smaller, a child again.

"Where're you going?" Callie would ask, and Jacob would tell her. "You haven't told anyone about our place, have you?"

"No ma'am," Jacob lied. He had told Drue, because he told Drue everything, but Callie liked to hear that she was the only one who knew and always asked, expecting each time to hear the same answer, which made her feel special to Jacob. And that part was not a lie.

Jacob squatted at the place where he used to sit. It was not what he thought it would be, this coming back. He had expected an elation which did not show itself, but neither did the nostalgia or the sadness he expected. There was, though, a calm satisfaction that enveloped him.

The valley was long, there was no disappointment there. But the houses seemed smaller and other things different in a strange way. As in looking at a piece of land, you know the trees, the swell of the land both familiar and new. Familiar because you were here long ago, new because you are here now. And you wonder why becoming a few years older or a few feet taller has made such a difference.

So you squat down to your size of eight or nine, and it is still not the same. You touch the roots of trees where you played or maybe just stand for a moment inside the scene, because there is something to be known or gotten from it. But you cannot grasp what it is. Then you think that what will be known will come up through the ground into your body where you stand, shooting a knowledge through your legs and you may learn something that could make you stand straight for the rest of your life. And you hope that is true and that that is the way it happens. But it isn't, so you touch the bark and lower yourself to sit on roots twisting out of the ground. You lean back, letting the curve of the roots wrap around your shoulders. And you wish they would reach all the way around like someone's arms.

You lay back into that tree for an hour or so, nothing to hear or say, only the feel of the bark at your shoulders and back. And when you leave you take it with you as you would take the tune of a favorite song heard at the beginning of a day that runs through your mind while you are working or sitting down to read.

Jacob walked back to town and realized that it was well past noon. Soldier had left from in front of the store and sat now on the steps of his apartment house across the street.

Jacob spoke to him as he walked by. Soldier looked up, startled, his whole face looking to Jacob.

"Hi, yourself," Soldier said, trying to make a joke.

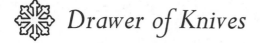 *Drawer of Knives*

In his room that night Jacob opened the drawer of the bedside table to put some things in it. His mother's diary was there. Annie had given it to Jacob earlier. She said, "Look through this, Jake. I want to ask you something about it." Then she brought it to his room and put it in the drawer. Her expression had been one he had never seen on her before, though he had seen the diary, and as a boy sneaked looks at it; but afraid of being caught he had always put it back before reading too much. As he opened it now, he saw in the front, his mother's name printed in bold black letters: SARAH. There were pages, weeks not filled in. He turned to February 1928.

Valentine's Day—February 14, 1928
Karl bought me a box of candy. We had a nice dinner and I fixed him what he likes. The children swapped valentines at school. Karl did not drink so much today. Maybe he is really trying to stop.

February 21, 1928
Karl drank for two days straight. It never fails to happen that when I decide things are all right that they begin to fall apart. The kids are beginning to ask if their daddy is drunk. Annie asked yesterday, then Drue asked. Jacob notices, but I don't think he understands exactly,

like when Karl doesn't hear him or answer him. I don't know what to tell Annie.

February 29, 1928
Jake was sick today, a terrible cough. I hope he is all right by Saturday which is his birthday. He will be four years old. Karl is doing better. I am pregnant, but wish I wasn't.

April 24, 1928
A spring day. So beautiful. The jonquils are full and my tulips are bright and colorful. Karl not drinking so much now. Things are all right. He's glad I'm pregnant and he took an extra job for the fall. He'll take a course at night at the college outside town. He has already started to prepare and reads all the time. His job at the mill is good, but I think it's never been what he really wants to do. He will be promoted though. He told me yesterday he will be the person in charge of getting lumber from all over the state. I asked if he would have to travel and he got mad. Said even if he did it wouldn't be that much. I didn't say anything else. He doesn't know how lonely I am.

When Jacob looked at the date of the last entry, he turned to the next year, fall of 1929, and scanned the pages. There was a tone of hopefulness until about Thanksgiving.

November 28, 1929
Thanksgiving came and went. We had a nice dinner, only couldn't help thinking of so many people who did not have enough food. The government is setting up places where people can get bread and other things. We will not have to stand in those lines, not yet at least. Karl says we must put aside our money, as much as we

66

can, because things will get worse, he says. I took our money out of the bank just in time. Some people couldn't get theirs, any of it. I couldn't get all of ours, but most of it. I put it in an envelope and stuck it in my underwear drawer. I will add to it whenever I can and I've told the children that I will not be buying them extra things now. I am very tired. It seems I get to bed later and later every night.

After this, there were days and weeks of sketchy entries, each one more worried than the last.

December 16, 1929
Karl drinking a lot. Maybe it's because of Christmas. I wish he would stop.

December 30, 1929
Nanna died today. She has lived with us for so long. We will miss her. I almost won't know what to do without her in that upstairs room.

Nanna was Karl's grandmother. She brought Karl to America just before the outbreak of the First World War. Karl was eighteen. His parents left him at an early age, so he lived with his grandmother, was raised by her hand. He never saw his parents except in a picture. He didn't know why.

It was spring when Nanna packed their last load into a friend's car. They would be taken to the boat, but Nanna had one more small trunk and she waited in the flat for Karl to come get her. A hat with a veil sat directly on top of her head and she stood up as Karl walked in. Nanna's hair was the color of iron. She had it tucked neatly under her hat. Beneath her arm was a dull-flowered satchel filled with letters and some jewelry she loved. Behind her was a piano they would have to leave.

She handed Karl a picture of herself. It was a recent photograph taken at a studio. She handed it to him as though she thought she might be leaving him instead of Germany, or maybe she thought she would not look the same somewhere else, so she had the picture made. When she handed it to him, Karl felt the permanence of their move.

Nanna pointed to the trunk indicating that Karl should carry it for her, but her back straightened more than he had ever remembered. Her cheeks drew inward, pulled down, and her eyes fell on distant objects. He borrowed what he needed from her face, then lifted the trunk onto his shoulders and followed her out.

Nanna, seated between Karl and the friend, smoothed her long dress and it brushed against her ankles as she situated her legs. She spoke of the house where she grew up, the fields around it, the hills, and as she did her face moved into an expression of a banished recollection. Then she said, "Set your mind to kindness," and there hung in the air a silence that fell flat. "Give it or take it," her hands flew up and fluttered in the space between them, "but don't let the day go by without it."

She had meant to say so much more, but found she didn't know much more than what she had just said. So she said nothing, and they rode beside her, bewildered, bound by her words.

Karl had never been away from Germany and he was glad now that he would not be away from this woman who sat next to him in the car, then on the boat, her grief welling up into a sound as coarse as a cough.

They climbed the plank to the boat, and Karl tried to think of a way to give her comfort; but instead she comforted him. She told him that the house in Tennessee would repeat the lines of their own house, the crops and fields appearing the same, the way an artist repeats lines trying to capture a scene in the manner his mind dictates, but taking a lifetime to do it.

Then she reached into her satchel and brought out a print by a Dutch painter. The lines were geared for depth.

And he understood what Nanna kept inside herself: a visual permanence that lived in the lines of what she saw, no matter where she saw it. And the repetition of those lines gave a connection she needed, so that wherever they went she took with her the places she loved and she felt at home. As they rode the train through the hills of Tennessee, the hills rose up fresh and flaunted wildflowers as far as they could see.

When they reached Sweetwater, the heat surprised them. Nanna held a scarf to her forehead and Karl shaded his eyes. The landscape made them alert, and Karl thought of the words spoken earlier about kindness. Then he lifted his head to an air that made him hungry for sausage and stewed cabbage.

January 1, 1930
Buried Nanna. She looked beautiful. Karl made sure she had on her black dress with the wide lace collar. She wore it so much during her last days, still going out places—to town, to church. She wanted to wear it each time she went out, even though sometimes it was too dressed up for where she wanted to go. It was like she knew she would die soon, so she wore it thinking that no one would have to bother, but could just put her into the grave as she was. She was like that, wanting to handle everything herself, not be a burden. But when she died, she died in her sleep and she wore a soft flannel nightgown. But her dress in the closet had just been cleaned, and the collar, a wide ecru, not white, made her face (when they dressed her in it), made her face seem softer and lifelike, more than anyone's face I've ever seen in death. She looked so beautiful. One thing I did. When I saw she didn't have on earrings, I took my own off and clipped them on her ears. I hope that was all right. She always wore earrings with

69

that dress and her ears without them looked bare, so I did that. Karl did not drink one single drop today.

Annie knocked at Jacob's door. "Jake? You still up?"

"Yes."

Annie came in. She saw the diary and put it on her lap. "What are you looking for?" She flipped the pages then turned back to where Jacob was reading.

"I don't know. Just reading it."

"Here's about the stillborn," she said.

"I saw that."

There had been four children born to Karl and Sarah. The last was a boy, born dead. Jacob did not even see his face, but he knew the waiting and anticipation. Aunts and uncles came to the house. Women cooked food and served strong coffee until late at night. Mason jars filled with peas and beans and tomatoes from summer were served up hot, giving the feeling that all was well, or building the atmosphere of a special occasion through the cooking of food that had been stored away. It was winter, and the steam that rose from the firm kernels of corn scraped in summer months gave the room an ambience of a holiday.

Jacob ushered the doctor into his mother's room and his mother told Jacob to wait in the kitchen. When the doctor left, he did not tell Jacob good-bye, but left by the back door carrying something in a blanket. The house became quiet and people sat at the table until steam no longer rose from the corn. When Jacob touched it with his hand, it was cold. And one of his aunts told him not to touch the corn.

Jacob guessed his mother must be sleeping, because everyone began to speak in whispers. His father sat in the living room, but he wanted no one in there with him. He did not light the lamp as it grew dark and he drank whatever anyone brought to him.

Jacob edged along the hallway to his mother's room. He hoped one of his aunts wouldn't see him, stop him. He wanted to see his mother and pushed open the door. He saw her propped up slightly. She was not asleep and her face looked like ashes. And though Jacob did not ask her anything, she shook her head no, indicating she didn't want to say more. But then she said, "Would you like to name him? We have to give him a name."

Jacob wanted to pronounce something worthy. He had learned the books of the Bible and was recently awarded a gold pin for his recitation. He could be awarded additional bars to hang on the pin if he learned other things: psalms, hymns, the Easter story. If he learned the catechism, he got a New Testament. But he wasn't to all that yet. He had learned only the names of the books. And the one most easy to remember was Ruth. But he couldn't name his brother Ruth, so he said Obadiah. And later everyone said they were glad he hadn't said Ruth. They told him it was a fine name he had chosen, except Annie and Drue, who told him it was stupid and why did he do that. Obadiah Bechner was carved on the gravestone.

Sarah stayed in bed for five weeks after her stillborn.

Jacob, Drue, and Annie waited for her to recuperate, but began to think that the recuperation period would never end. Karl took over the household chores and the cooking, but Jacob was only four and wanted his mother to fix dinner, not his father. As the children played their nighttime game of marbles on the floor, Karl stepped around them and patted each one's head. At some point he would ask their help with dinner, so they hurried to finish their game, each one trying to win the blue marble. It was what the marble game was all about, the streaked marble, streaked blue and white-blue. Every marble game was about that blue one.

Their father lit the stove and adjusted the knob until the flame was right, then he turned to open a drawer of knives. The

71

drawer was stuck, so he jerked and shook it and finally with both hands he yanked it loose. The children shifted with surprise and turned to see what their minds would see for years, holding the image of their father and the drawer of knives exploding into the air, then crashing around them in a rain to the floor. No one was hurt.

Sarah hurried downstairs to see the room showered with metal, the knives scattered around the children's legs. Karl still held the drawer with both hands letting it hang in front of his knees, a quiet shade.

The children looked to Sarah in the doorway. She wore her nightgown which they had never seen her in without her robe. She covered her breasts with her arms, then stepped to Karl to lift the drawer from his hands, and she rolled it into place. She motioned for the children to pick up the knives. They arranged them exactly as they had been, in separate compartments the way Sarah preferred.

Sarah took butter from the larder, some eggs and cream. She began to cook for the first time in weeks, breakfast, though it was nighttime. And the lights against the dark windows held a glow which in their own hearts reflected relief. Karl ate and asked for seconds. Annie and Drue did the same. Jacob ate, though he was not hungry.

He stared at his mother's nightgown which was low-cut enough to see the large wide crease her bosom made, and he could see too, the handkerchief, lacy and white, that she kept tucked inside, nestled there like it was a small white flower.

And the night Jacob's own son was born, Joseph, he stood in the waiting room of a hospital in Virginia, and he remembered another wait. So that when the door swung open and a nurse in a green cap and face mask handed a child to him, wrapped in a small hospital blanket, she said. "It's a boy. You have a boy. What will you name him? Your wife told me to ask."

72

Jacob held the wrapped blanket close and awkward to his body and he thought how long he had waited, since four years old, to be shown this face.

Annie turned to a place in the diary, a few years earlier from where Jacob was reading. She read out loud.

October 17, 1925
Callie is better today. She says she wishes people would come by to see her. She's still in the hospital. She says nobody comes by to see her, but Ruben and me and sometimes Karl. She doesn't know why. People have been talking, saying how awful it was. What happened. I try to tell them that Callie is all right and that she was awfully scared. They shake their heads, and I can't tell if they are sorry for her or dismissing her. I see a bad thing happening. I must stay a friend to her. Nanna says I must let her come over here and that we must not close her out.

Annie kept reading, distracted, looking for something.

October 23, 1925
Callie is out of the hospital. I told her she could come over here anytime. She wants to come on Sunday since that's my birthday. I will be 30. I am six years younger than Callie. I didn't know that before. We are becoming good friends. Ruben is nice too. He and Karl have started talking about going hunting. That's in a few weeks. Maybe Callie will stay with me while they're gone. She doesn't have children and seems to like mine.

Annie looked to Jacob, but didn't say anything. She was not reading what she had wanted to read. Then she found the section she was looking for. "Oh, here it is," she told him.

October 31, 1925

The children dressed in their Halloween costumes and walked around tonight. Callie walked with them part of the way, but got tired and came back to the house. Ruben and Karl spent the evening cleaning their guns. Callie and me answered the door for the trick or treaters. And I told my whole story to Callie tonight. I have never told it before. Not even when I was young. I didn't mention it even then to anybody.

November 2, 1925

I told Callie again today. We talked. She's a good listener and it feels so good to say what has been kept quiet all these years. Callie doesn't think any less of me for it.

Annie looked up. "What did mother tell Callie?"

"I don't know." It was the first Jacob had heard of it. "Doesn't it say somewhere in there?"

"No. I've looked for it. It's not in here."

"Callie would know," Jacob told her.

"Well, I guess. If she can remember. But she's so old. Wait 'til you see her. She still recognizes people and will recognize you, I'm sure. She wants to see you."

Jacob took the diary and read to himself.

November 5, 1925

The men went hunting for a week. Callie comes over every day. I am glad we have talked. All these years I have wanted someone to tell this to. Nanna asked if Callie wanted to stay with us until the men got back, and I think she will do it. She is wonderful with the children. Jake especially likes her. She holds him on her lap until he is asleep. I am afraid that when she leaves he will be awfully spoiled.

Drawer of Knives

November 9, 1925
We went shopping today. Had fun. Callie even laughed
and seemed cheerful. I think she's going to be all right.
Nanna thinks so too. People still are not friendly to her
though. And she might lose her job. I wanted to say again
my whole story, or else just talk about it. But I didn't. I
think she might get tired of hearing it. But it does me
good.

November 11, 1925
We will be glad to see the men come back, though they
have decided to stay a few more days. It's nice to be here
with Nanna and Callie, but I wouldn't want a steady diet
of it. Callie has gotten quiet again. I think it's because
she's afraid she might lose her job. She teaches fifth
grade.

"When did you last see her?" Jacob asked.
"A few days ago. I told her you were here, and would come
to see her. She said she thought you would."

November 15, 1925
The men got home today. Two deer were shot, but Karl
didn't get one, neither did Ruben. They'll go back in
December.

November 20, 1925
Callie lost her job. They didn't give her much of a reason.
They had been looking for someone else and when they
found another teacher they made up some excuse to let
Callie go. She came over. She and Ruben stayed for dinner. Ruben said that maybe they should move away, because of what happened. But me and Karl want them to
stay. Ruben has his store and all.

75

"Well," Jacob said and closed the diary, put it back into the drawer. He took out the letter Callie had written to him and gave it to Annie. Annie looked at the handwriting. "It's hard to read," she said, so Jacob read it to her.

Jacob did not get out the clipping.

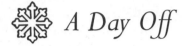 *A Day Off*

On Friday afternoon Cedar and Ty called Annie's house to tell Jacob what time they would be ready for the circus. Jacob said he would be there, but he was a little late.

The circus had already begun when they arrived, the elephants lumbering around the circle once to show themselves. The youngest was sitting, an easy trick. Jacob pointed to the man waiting at the side entrance with a wheelbarrow. He held a huge broom and can of powdered disinfectant.

"How'd you like to have his job?" Jacob asked.

Ty shook his head a firm no.

"I wouldn't mind it so much," Cedar told them.

On the high wire a boy was getting ready to perform. A woman with glittery stockings and a sequined bathing suit stood in the middle ring. Cedar, Ty, and Jacob sat in the front row. One clown almost gave Cedar a balloon, but instead handed it to the girl behind her. Cedar went to Jacob, so Jacob motioned to the clown that he give her something. The clown handed her the string to a balloon with another balloon inside it. Cedar held it for a while, then gave it to Ty.

The elephants were herded off to the tune of "I Could Have Danced All Night," and the tightrope act was introduced. There were acts of juggling and daredevil tricks going on at the same time. The children ate popcorn and waited patiently for the people to get through with their tricks, so the animals could come out.

Cedar favored the large cats, but they both loved the elephants, their size and their stupid walk. When they came back in, Cedar clapped loudly and Ty cheered.

The elephant act was almost over when one elephant, the largest, maybe the oldest, reared up at the end of the tent. All eyes turned, thinking maybe this was his best trick. He made a loud noise. The master of ceremonies struggled with the reins pulling the elephant down, and the woman in the sequined bathing suit screamed and fell off his back. The man at the wheelbarrow rolled her out of the way of the elephant's feet. Three men pulled now at the reins, one in back used a whip, yelled Hyaah, to make him mind.

The people's laughter stopped, so did the band playing the waltz the elephants did tricks to. It was so quiet that for a minute it seemed more like church than circus. And people moved to the edges of their seats ready to bolt upward.

The elephant then lurched forward, kicking down, then stepping on one man whose chest was crushed in one blow without time for a last cry, and the elephant ran to the other side of the tent, his eyes looking at the crowd, more afraid, Jacob thought, than they were. The crowd rose up almost in one move, before they scattered. But the elephant knocked against a pole, snapped it in two, and the tent collapsed on one side, falling soft like a burlap bag. Jacob huddled the children to him. They stood looking to leave. Men tried to get the other elephants out of the tent, since they too might imitate their oldest leader. The oldest leader could not be calmed, but continued to rear up and the circus workers surrounded him, throwing a net larger than anything Jacob had ever seen around his back and neck.

Over the loudspeaker, a crackling voice asked people to sit down, and Jacob could see people scrambling to rescue the dead man. Another pole was substituted for the one that broke, so that the tent was back up again, if not the same.

"What will they do?" Cedar asked Jacob.

"They'll take the elephant back to his stall. He'll be all right."

But Jacob could see the circus keepers back a boxcar to the exit of the tent. And a team of men drove and pulled the already netted animal into it. As people watched, they calmed themselves. Inside the boxcar the animal began to kick and scream, as though for help, as though in apology to say he meant no harm, but wanted rest, or a day off.

The men pulled the boxcar from the exit, and Jacob and the children followed to see where they would roll it. The band started playing and trapeze artists came out, pretending nothing had happened. The man at the wheelbarrow huddled over the sequined woman.

Several others had followed the boxcar, walking behind it, a procession, as it was pulled along to a clearing. It was seven o'clock, and the woods behind them were completely dark, but the clearing held its own light a little longer than the woods, and Jacob could see, if not everything, at least the shadows of people moving.

"Stand back," Jacob told the children and the people standing next to him, as the circus keepers threw gasoline onto the sides of the boxcar and poured thick puddles beneath it. The boxcar rocked and moved with a cradled force, the animal inside pushing with his weight against the strong wood. As a match was thrown, a whoof of air blew up into a soft explosion, and the band inside the tent played louder, a faster song. Some more people gathered, but stood back from the heat and squinted against the tall light.

The children had not spoken a word, but stood beside Jacob, not quite believing. Thinking that in a moment the elephant would exit unscathed, that it would be a trick everyone laughed and clapped for.

The man standing beside Jacob had on overalls, shoes worn too many years, and a hat not bought for him, but his now. Jacob recognized the old soldier's coat. "Hello, Soldier," Jacob said, wanting to do anything but look at that boxcar. Soldier did not avert his gaze, but stared as though hypnotized by the flames, and his smooth face was rough, even in that light. And for some reason Jacob felt like making a joke, wanting to say something that would make Soldier laugh. But he sensed he couldn't, so they stood together and waited.

The cries of the elephant had started now. He could be heard for miles. The band stopped its playing and in town people lifted their heads, thinking they must be dreaming to hear such a cry. Even to the closest town, the animal's shrill voice could be heard, for miles and miles. And for years the children carried the cry with them.

When they got home, they told their mother about the animal in the boxcar, though Ty told the most. And as he told, Verna cradled herself with her own arms and rocked back and forth.

They spent the night at Annie's house; but that night, later, Cedar went to Jacob's room. She knocked on his door. It was very late. She said, "It was a terrible thing they did." She wore Albert's shirt and some slippers that looked like rabbits.

"Yes. It was."

"Why did they do it? Burn him like that?"

"They were afraid. People do things when they're afraid."

"I wouldn't do that," she said, but her eyes weren't sure whether or not she would do something similar.

"I know you wouldn't."

She said she had to go to bed, and walked down the hallway. Albert's shirttail hung at her knees.

Molly called Jacob the next morning.

"What happened?" Molly asked.

"What do you mean?"

"Didn't you see Callie yet?"

"No."

Her silence indicated she was puzzled. "Why not?"

Jacob began to tell of the circus incident, and Cedar and
Ty, and he told of the people he had seen at Sophie's and Ned's,
and finally of Soldier who was still around. "Can you believe
he's still here?"

"I thought he'd be dead."

"Everybody thought so by now," said Jacob. "He outlived
his uncle."

"I'll be." Molly didn't know whether or not to mention Callie
again. "Jake?" she said.

"What?" He didn't offer anything.

"Annie and Albert okay?"

"Yes." He began to tell of the hunting trip a week away.

"They still throw a big dance to send everybody off?"

Jacob told her they did.

"Well," said Molly, "then you'll see Callie this week, I
guess." It was a question.

Silence. Jacob didn't know why he was silent. "I will, but
don't keep asking me about it, Molly." He laughed to hide his
irritation, but it was more a breath through his nose than a
laugh.

"You call me when you feel like it." Molly ended their conversation.

Jacob said he would, and when he hung up the phone he
left the house.

Jacob had been back to Sweetwater many times during the
early years of their marriage when he and Molly first moved
to Virginia. He came for hunting trips. Sometimes he brought
Molly and the children and they might stay a week or two if
it was summer and the children were still young. But his returns had lessened some after the death of his father, then even
more after Sarah died. Sarah died of old age. It was easy and
expected, and Sarah had even asserted that she was "ready" to
die, had been ready for years. Though in her last few moments,
Jacob felt her expression belied that assertion.

Whenever he returned he would visit their graves. Annie went with him, expected him to go each time he returned. So Jacob stopped returning, because Drue's grave was next to his mother's and father's. And though Jacob couldn't explain it, he felt that people knew more in death than they knew in life, so that standing above the three graves he felt that they knew even more than he himself knew, and he could not look down on them, could not visit, or even come back to Sweetwater.

Annie asked him yesterday if he wanted to "visit the graves" but Jacob told her he had already done that, then increased his lie by saying, "I've been out there twice, Annie."

"Well," said Annie, "I would've gone with you," and her statement seemed final, as though she might not suggest it again.

Before, when Jacob returned, when the children were still young, nothing was ever said about Drue. It was something in the past people remembered, but didn't talk about. Oh, sometimes someone might say "I wish Drue could see Tom. Tom Bechner looks just like Drue, don't you think?" And Jacob agreed that Tom looked more like Drue than like himself. "Though Joseph looks just like you," they told him, "the very image." And Jacob was proud of his first son who looked so much like himself.

Jacob had often wondered what Molly thought about the night Drue died. He had never asked her, but instead suffered periods of withdrawal. Molly called those periods "chair-sitting." "Daddy's chair-sitting," the children would say. It was considered a phase, much like a teenager might go through. Jacob wondered how he would end the phase. He almost asked Molly once, and in fact he did say "What do you think happened? How did Drue's house catch fire?"

"He was probably sleeping," Molly told him, "or listening to music and dozed off. He just didn't wake up soon enough, and when he did his clothes had already caught."

Jacob held a gun. He remembered that. He remembered
Drue coming around the corner, but Drue was already hurt by
then. And Jacob didn't remember stepping into the room and
doing that to him. One thing he knew, he knew he had heard
a gun go off, and had heard it for years as it came back to his
mind like the sound of a bell, reminding, sending him to his
chair.

But when Joseph died, Jacob learned to show sadness in a
different way, more openly. For a while he thought that this
loss was his retribution. He thought he had lost his son, because of what he had done to his brother, and though his grief
was not comparable to anything he had ever experienced, still
he felt that maybe it was something he deserved. While he
believed in the retribution, he was able to show his sadness
more openly; but then after a few months his old habit returned and Molly found him again in his chair.

Jacob had been surprised to receive the letter from Callie,
but not shocked really. Instead he felt anticipation and maybe
even a hope of relief, maybe an end to the chair-sitting. And
while he did not articulate in his mind what she might tell him,
he felt as though he had been waiting a long time for her to
send for him.

But now, after being here ten days and having more days to
go before the hunt, after taking Cedar and Ty everywhere,
and planning the hunt with Albert and Ned in the diner at
night, seeing almost everyone but Callie, he couldn't help but
question (as Molly had) his procrastination, and feel irritated
by it. He did not know what he would do if Callie accused
him of what all these years he had accused himself.

All Jacob wished, all he ever wished was for things to be
different.

Jacob had walked almost a mile since leaving the house.
He wished now he had not spoken sharply to Molly, but he

83

wasn't really thinking of Molly. He wasn't thinking of Callie either. He was thinking of Drue.

He could see off the road the old schoolhouse that had housed him from kindergarten to sixth grade. No one used it now. The schoolhouse door lay propped open with a broken broom handle stuck deliberately beneath it. The floor of the room buckled and rotted and two large size rats scooted across the floor and hid behind some loose boards.

A globe on a wooden stand stood in the corner, and school desks lay scattered about the room. There was no order. Jacob remembered the globe, how he loved to spin it when he was exactly its size. He would spin and stop it with his finger, deciding wherever his finger landed that that would be the place he might live someday. His finger stopped the globe so many times, but the only time he remembered was whenever it landed on a place called Lucknow, because he knew someone by that name, or on another place in India near the Himalayas, because he had heard of the Himalayas. Out of all the spins that globe took, that was the place he chose to remember and he looked for it now. He brushed away the dust and thought how he would plan the spin and guide his finger to land on that place.

This was his fifth grade room where he had loved Mary Lou Jenkins. All the boys had loved Mary Lou at least once during the first through sixth grades. Jake, though, had loved her the longest. His love lasted almost the entire year. As he thought of her, he felt a little of the old queasiness return.

Mary Lou Jenkins sat beside Jacob in the lunchroom and on the bus she saved a seat for him. He called her sometimes at night, taking his father's telephone as far as it would reach into his own room. On Saturdays, every Saturday in fact for several months, they went skating together. They held hands by crossing their arms in front, the way he would see real skaters do. Jake knew that without Mary Lou he would never skate so well, and he was right. It was the only time in his life he attempted skating of any kind.

But just before spring, about March, Drue (who was an eighth-grader by then) began to show deliberate interest in Mary Lou. Jacob would see Mary Lou talking to him, then Drue began to meet her after school in front of the junior high. Soon they began to go to the drugstore for a cherry smash. Mary Lou's curls bobbed as she walked. Jacob didn't mention to anyone how he felt, instead he told his friends how glad he was that Drue had a girl and that even though Mary Lou was probably too young for Drue that still it was a good thing. And he said this as though Drue might be less fortunate because of his birthmark. But he couldn't be sure people understood what he meant or how he meant it, so sometimes he added, "You know," and then the person would nod, but still he wasn't sure if he had put his point across. Finally, he just let it go.

Jacob fingered the globe, and though he didn't spin it a feeling of the possibility of exotic travel was brought back anyway. He found the Himalayas, then Lucknow, but instead of exuberance he felt a sick remorse, and thought that his faults were so much greater than other people's. He felt the path of his song deepening. Mary Lou Jenkins had not entered Jacob's mind in thirty years. Upon stepping out of the schoolhouse, Jacob felt an urge to run. He didn't know why. He didn't run, but let his feet pick up speed as he walked around the building. As Jacob hurried, he tripped over branches blown down by a previous storm. At first he thought it might be another cowbone, but when he fell he fell so completely that his arms could not break the fall and his face hit a branch. Another branch stuck into his leg. The fall had seemed to take a long time, and as he pushed up, the getting up came slowly too, all of it, the falling and the getting up done in a few moments' time, but the falling seemed years and the getting up more like long drawn out days of sickness. He wondered, because of Mary Lou and other things, if he had ever loved his brother.

Before he stood up a voice came from above him. "What're you doing?" It was Ty.

"Nothing. I just fell."

Behind Ty stood two other boys. Jacob could tell they came here often, claimed the schoolhouse as their own.

"That's our club," one boy told Jacob, implying, Jacob thought, possession and ownership and the implication that Jacob was not allowed here.

"That's where I used to go to school." Jacob stood and brushed himself off.

All three boys turned as though they thought Jacob might be much older than they had imagined.

"Here?" One boy stepped forward. "You went to school here?"

"It looked better then," Jacob defended.

They walked to the side entrance of the schoolhouse and stopped. The boys wanted Jacob to leave them now, let them get down to business. They waited, the way their parents might wait after spending all day with children, but now suddenly wanting to be alone.

Jacob told them good-bye. The boys stood until he walked away. He guessed they thought he might fall again and wondered what he looked like, falling. He still did not feel as though he had risen all the way to a standing position.

But one thing he noticed: he was no longer thinking of Drue.

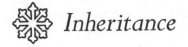 # Inheritance

There were times when Jacob was a young boy that his family took trips through all the southern states. Jacob liked the traveling, but what he liked most was telling later about the states they had traveled. There was no particular destination, only the traveling, and trying to see how many state lines they could cross.

When Jacob rode on those trips, he would turn his head to watch the trees and fields that went by. Sometimes when he looked, as he turned his head, there was a moment, but only one moment, when he saw something he recognized, a space in the trees that hung above the ground; and he saw both the space and the ground, and the light on it. It was a clearing he thought he had seen before, even played in. Not déjà vu so much, not a trick the mind plays because the place where memory is stored goes faster than what is happening in the present, but a knowledge that is deeper than anything learned so far in life. So Jacob would ask his father as they rode, "Who owns that land?" because he didn't know what else to ask. And his father would point to a farmhouse and say, "That man there, I guess." Jacob would envy the man who owned it. Then he would lean trying to see it again before it was out of sight.

And Jacob understood why there are times when you pass some trees or a piece of land that takes your eye, that that land even seems to call, make you hear something; but upon closer inspection it falls from you so that you feel a loss. Then you lean toward it as if you might find what you have missed, knowing it is important. But still, you feel a loss, because the whole seeing and hearing was within you and momentary, and there was no way to prolong the pleasure of it. And when your mother sees you leaning and asks you what it is you see, you wouldn't know. It was like that.

During those trips, Jacob's father told the story of his immigration. But he had told the story so many times that the children could mouth it behind his back as they rode in the car. "This summer," Karl would say, "we will travel farther," but they only did that once. "It will not be the first time I have traveled so far," and Karl would begin his story. "When I was eighteen," he said, his expression one of someone who had just entered a vast hall. The children settled back to let the wind blow their hair. They mouthed places in the story they knew best, turning to each other at different times to mouth closely into each other's faces. Karl would not notice.

"Now, Karl, let's stop here," Sarah would say and Karl stopped, or did anything Sarah wanted, because she made those decisions: where to stop, where to eat. And if Jacob or Drue or Annie saw something that might be fun, they could turn to their mother and ask if they could stop and Sarah usually said Yes.

Each time they entered a new state, Karl announced it. "Okay. Here's one. South Carolina." Then later. "Here's Georgia," as if he were handing it to them on a platter.

"Looks just like Tennessee," Jacob said.

Jacob expected to look up and find a marked difference as they crossed the state line, and he complained when he couldn't see the line. He and Drue stuck their heads out the window so the wind could catch their hair, blow it on all sides. But Jacob kept his eyes ready for a clearing, something along the road that might speak to him. He leaned like the barley fields in

Tennessee. Sometimes he longed to stop, to find the clearing he had seen, to walk in it, make it his own.

And it was on those trips that Jacob heard the history of his father's life, his father's Nanna, his father's absent parents. Jacob heard over and over a history told to all of them, though Jacob seemed to listen the most.

He even asked questions. Drue and Annie barely listened (they had been listening for more years), until their father mentioned what they might inherit. But there was nothing to inherit, it was only the word (inheritance) that made them listen. For what Karl told them they would have were things he had already given to them.

What would be theirs, he told them, was a watch that belonged to Karl's father. The watch would be Drue's. The shawl of Nanna's would be Annie's, and the hairbrush. Annie had had those things for two years. One picture that belonged to no one was given collectively to remind them where they came from. But the children knew nothing about the people in the picture, because Karl knew nothing about them either. The picture was of a young couple (Karl's own parents): the man smiling, though he looked as if smiling did not come natural to him, the woman handing him a jar of jam or relish. She was barefoot. Karl carried the picture in his wallet and took it out on trips, fumbling as he drove the car to bring it out, show it again and let the sepia figures tell what they could.

"I never knew them, but needed to know them at times." If Karl were drinking, he might grow teary. "But I don't resent them anymore." He said the part about not resenting, usually repeating it several times. And later when he began to drink, he told in a slurry tongue how he didn't resent it, until Sarah said that if he had resented it some, maybe he wouldn't have to drink so much.

"Jacob," he would finally get to what would be Jacob's, but Jacob at the age of seven had already received it, and wasn't all that happy with his inheritance. "Jacob gets the eyeglasses that belonged to Nanna, and her satchel."

Jacob used the satchel in school. The flowers on it had faded enough to look more like ancient hieroglyphics than flowers. Sometimes his father told him they were figures in a primitive war. Jacob didn't care much for the eyeglasses, but he liked the steel rims and thick glass. And he noticed that whenever he looked through them, everything blurred, but as years went by he found as he tried them on that objects grew more clear. So his vision cleared when he put them on and blurred when he took them off. He liked the idea that his sight was failing in the same way hers had, but he hoped he had inherited some of her strengths as well as her weakness.

"What we finally come down to," Karl said as he finished bequeathing, "What we finally come down to," and here he held up one finger, "a hairbrush, a watch, a pair of old eyeglasses, things we used every day, not special things," he let his hand drop, "but necessary." Then if any of the children happened to be riding in the front seat, between the parents, Karl would put his arm around that child and give a hug. "Ja!" he would say. And whoever sat there (Drue or Annie or Jacob) liked it, because if Karl did anything well it was this. He held people not in a short preemptive way; but completely, making the person seem more needed than anyone else. Even neighbor children liked those hugs that Karl gave and would wait through all the talking to receive one.

If none of the children sat in the front seat beside him, Karl would turn in the car to tell the children one last thing, and as he did, the car would swerve and Sarah would say, "Karl! Pay attention!" So Karl faced the road again, but the children listened more attentively.

"You will have to decide," said Karl, "what you will keep to remind you that I was here."

What Jacob kept was the label of a Robert Burns cigar.

90

November 17, 1930
Told Callie again today. Haven't told her in a long time.
I could sense that she was getting tired as soon as I
began the story of it. But it has been on my mind. What
I did. And even though I was young and didn't really
know what I was doing, still, it is a hard thing. Karl and
Ruben went hunting today. Me and Callie and the chil-
dren will have a picnic tomorrow if it's not too cold.
Today was nice.

Jacob looked through his mother's diary each night,
glancing, not reading everything, but searching for whatever
she had told to Callie. Cedar and Ty called to thank him for
letting them sleep in the piano box.
"Thanks for taking us, and for the circus," Ty said. He
meant it, but wouldn't have thought to call and say it.
"Yes," Cedar echoed. The thanks sounded forced, required
by Verna. Then "You left your sweater over here."
"I'll get it tomorrow."
Jacob asked to speak to Verna. She was standing near,
close to the children. "I left my sweater," Jacob said. He
wanted to say something else. "Ty talked in his sleep, the
night we stayed outside."
"I know. Cedar told me."
"Does he *know* his father?"
"Not really. Just the name."
"That's what he called out."
"I know. He does that sometimes."
"Well, I just wanted to tell you."
When the phone rang again, Annie answered it downstairs.
Jacob hoped Molly might call tonight. He turned to December
10, 1930, and pictured his mother sitting down to write.

Whenever I talk to Callie, she says what I did doesn't
matter and that I must forget about it. When she says it,

91

and the way she says it, makes me think that maybe I
could, maybe I can. Forget about it. Maybe I can really
do that. Callie is able to forget a lot—I mean, the way
people have treated her, still treat her. She forgets,
though no one else does. I do not know anyone like Callie
Belden Locke. She is my best friend.

December 16, 1930
The men went on their second deer hunt yesterday, but
they brought Karl home today. All the way from deer
camp. I think they were mad at him. I sure was. He got
drunk and cut his hand on a kitchen knife. Not too bad,
but he had to have it bandaged. He'll go back to the camp
tomorrow. I wish he would stop drinking.

Jacob flipped pages, whole sections, until he turned to
March 7, 1943:

Drue is dead. How can I hold together. He burned in a
fire. Annie is here. Jake is here. Karl did not drink so
much today.

And the next day:

I went to identify Drue's body. Karl went with me. It
felt like some horrible dream to walk down those stairs
into that place, to see Drue laid out, almost not recogniz-
able. Karl was wonderful though. He was my strength
down there in that place. I don't know what I would have
done if he had not been with me to answer everything
and make the arrangements. Tomorrow Drue will be
buried and the next week Karl said we would take a trip.
A thing we haven't done in a long time.

Jacob tried to remember what trip they had taken.

April 14, 1943
A beautiful spring day. Drue. Drue. You were my favorite and the most trouble to me.

May 5, 1943
Nothing today.

Then there were weeks with no entry at all. Only blank pages until July and Jacob's wedding.

July 17, 1943
Jake and Molly married today. We were glad. Molly looked beautiful in her dress. They have a house on Garrett Road and Jake has a job at the lumber mill. But Molly told me today they might move to Virginia. I wish she hadn't told me that today. Drue dead now four months.

In the fall Jacob and Molly moved to Virginia.

Sept. 11, 1943
Jake and Molly moved to Virginia. Jake took a teaching job there. It won't pay as much as what he made here in the mill and I don't see why he had to go but he was bent on leaving, so I finally just wished them well. I have Annie here. Karl too, but Karl's not much company to me anymore. He stays in his room now all morning, not coming out until almost one o'clock. I'm sleeping in the extra room off the porch. I don't know what will become of Karl. I don't know what will become of me.

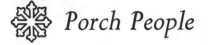 *Porch People*

Jacob was not drafted until 1944. In fact, both Drue and Jacob were not selected for draft because Karl was German. No one mentioned this reason though. They had been able to avoid the War because the local draft board juggled the names in a way that kept them unavailable for service, or at least postponed their time. It was Drue's death, and the publicity of it, that finally brought the Bechner name forward. Jacob was called to service, but the War was almost over, and after only a year, he returned to Virginia.

There were bands and crowds parading a busload of soldiers through the streets. Men gathered into formation because people seemed to want them to march as if a parade had been planned.

Jacob saw Molly and Joseph on the curb. As Molly ran to Jacob, he broke out of line. One man with higher rank motioned for Jacob to get back into formation, but it was too late. For at the same moment, other women ran to meet their men and the formation collapsed as surely as if it had been held taut by a rope that was suddenly or irrevocably cut.

Joseph was still an infant and didn't recognize his father. Jacob's skin looked baked, his stride had slackened into a slow movement, and he had a coarseness that stayed with him through life. Joseph cried and clung to his mother's dress. When Jacob took him, he hit his father's shoulders, two flat palms pounding a hard greeting.

They went home to a dinner of chicken and rice, black-eyed peas with bits of ham, and large hot rolls. After Joseph was in bed, Molly brought out fresh strawberries and served them to Jacob with coffee and a bottle of brandy she saved until now. They built a fire, which was not needed since it was already spring. But a quick rain had come while they were eating and the air was cool. The windows opened to the breeze and the fire felt good to them.

When Molly sat on the floor, she leaned against Jacob's knees and he felt a sudden discomfort. He wanted to tell Molly all that had happened, how it didn't matter. He wanted to tell how he was ill on the side of the road in France, how some-one lifted him onto a truck bed, propped two boards to block the wind from his face and took him to their farmhouse. A doctor came to check on him; a woman and young girl cared for him.

Jacob regained his strength slowly, and, as he grew strong-er, tried to help with small chores. The man who found him was the only one in the household who spoke English. His name was Girard. He was twenty years older than Jacob, his neck already stringy with age. He was a stout man with the beginnings of a paunch. His face had long since lost its youth, his cheeks engraved by hard winters. But in his veins ran a fiber tougher than blood.

Girard's wife was a large woman, and though she wasn't as large as Girard, she seemed to be. Her skin lay smoothed by a layer of fat that pressed all over her body and ironed out wrinkles that age should have put there. Their daughter, Nicole, was seventeen. Jacob loved to watch her move around the house. She moved like a deer, and each time he turned to see her again, she was gone.

Nicole's quick movements from the yard to the table enter-tained Jacob's days and when he was well enough to work outside, the girl followed him, stood close enough sometimes to rub against his shoulder. And at these times, Jacob could breathe in the smell of her hair, soft curls that sat on her head like a cap.

Each morning when Jacob cleaned the stalls and fed the horses, Nicole followed him. One morning he found her in a fresh stall, her clothes lying beside her in a neat pile.

"Come here," she said. It was the only English she had spoken. She lay sprawled on the hay. Her legs made a triangle, her arms reached back over her head. Jacob decided the pose was a good one. She motioned for him to close both the top and the lower doors to the stall and when Jacob didn't move to do so, got up to close them herself. Her body was heavy with curves and she grew playful, pulling Jacob down, unbuttoning his shirt, saying, "Come here, Ja-cob." And he fell on her and took her just the way she wanted.

Every morning when he came to the stall, he found her there. So he took what she gave, until one morning she left for school in another town and showed no more interest in him. Jacob found that after a few weeks, he didn't miss her.

Molly leaned harder against his knees, but he said nothing so she didn't either. She didn't even face him, so he watched her profile, her long brown hair and her full mouth, her thin nose. He reached to put his hand on her breast and the warmth of her skin was almost hot. He undressed her before the fire and stared as he had when he saw her for the first time. He undressed himself and found that when he removed his own clothes, he felt embarrassed at his thinness. And as he stood before her, he asked what she thought. But Molly didn't answer.

"Can you touch this?" he said, and offered himself.

"I can do more than that." And Molly reached to stroke his legs, his arms and to cup him rising in her hands.

When he entered her, she clung to him, wrapping her legs high onto his back and taking his mouth with her own. And he felt the pressure of her waiting's hold on him. He moved with her and watched her finish above him, then again beneath him. And when he came inside her, he shuddered as if he were releasing a flock of doves.

Today was November the 12th. In two more days the hunting trip would begin. Jacob had not yet talked to Callie. He went to sit on the porch. It was too cold, but Jacob sat there anyway. This porch seemed to him another ground, or time.

The screen at the top of the porch had come loose, and Jacob remembered that the screens were loose (but only beginning to be loose) when he was a boy and sat on the porch at night when porch people gathered in the spring and summer to tell stories. The telling would start soon after supper, so that it involved a change of light, and affected the telling. Jacob would stare at the place where the screen was pulling out. Now almost all of it was pulled out, and he thought of the people who came on those nights.

There were some who waited to tell their story after it was dark, or waited until the shadows lengthened sufficiently or until the only light was the porch light that shone across the day bed and suffused the children with a kind of glow that showed all their wigglings and pushings and elbowings, so that the day bed on those nights had the effect of a beehive or a nest of worms.

Many stories were repeated year to year, embellished. Upon the completion of a story, there were appropriate lulls, voices flared and died. One night during a lull, when the porch light showed the children, Sarah told everyone how she met Karl. It was the first and only story she told.

"I met him on a riverbank," Sarah told. "Fishing." She spoke above the sounds of tree frogs. There was still some sunlight left, but it had changed from yellow to deep white, a twilight in which people could see each other, but not always recognize. "I knew how to fish, but Karl didn't even have a pole that first day." No one was looking at Sarah, but found parts of the porch to stare at. "He just sat there, but the next day he had a pole." She shifted to fold her legs beneath herself. "It was on a Sunday afternoon, that next day, I mean. I fixed sandwiches, some deviled eggs. I wrapped dill pickles in waxed paper, and poured lemonade into a clean milk bottle. Then," and the giving of the menu made the day bed rustle, "I cut thin slices of ham and thick slices of bread, some cheese, and made a salad layered with potatoes and sweet red onion. I drenched it with a dressing I made up myself, but couldn't tell you now what it was, if I had to. I placed two huge pieces of cake, still warm, at the bottom of the basket." She paused to remember something she had never forgotten. "When I got to the place on the riverbank where Karl had been the day before, he was already there, fishing.

"I told him I hoped he had some luck and spread my blanket down beside his new tackle box. He looked at the picnic basket and I said 'There's plenty,' which is what he wanted to know—you know, whether or not he was invited to stay or should leave. Then his line tugged and from his reaction I knew he was not a fisherman, maybe had never fished in his life, so I reached to reel it in or help him reel it in. The fish was big, a bass. Eight pounds maybe." The men on the porch looked up, caught interest. "As we brought it out, I reached to pull the hook and Karl grabbed my hips, caught me, because I had almost fallen into the water. We put the fish into the bucket."

Sarah smoothed her dress with the heels of her hands, she smoothed it often as she told the story. As the light faded, they could see only Sarah's arms and elbows moving against the pressure of her hands. "It was the first and only fish we caught that day, though there were other days." She turned to smile at Karl. Everyone stared at their object or found another one to look on. Karl lifted his drink and smiled into it.

Karl remembered how Sarah almost fell. He could see the

line of her legs beneath her dress; they rose like pillars in front of him. He could smell her fresh soapy smell and when he looked up could see her breasts dancing inside her blouse. His hands burned to touch her. He caught hold of her hips, not really catching her, but almost making her slip into the water. But she thanked him and put the fish into the bucket. He suggested they have lunch.

Sarah unwrapped the fat bread and cheese and thin slices of ham. She built sandwiches, then offered him a pickle and the jar of potato salad with a fork. Karl held up one potato drenched in the thick sauce, closing his eyes with the taste of it. When he saw at the bottom of the basket two large slices of chocolate cake, he decided he was probably in love with her.

She poured lemonade from the bottle. His eyes didn't leave her face, but swept over her as if he were painting her features, every one with a fine brush. Before the day was over, he would take her (and the blanket) further into the woods. He would remove her skirt and blouse. She would let him. He would not enter her then, not that day, but months later on a hot July night, he would enter her, jolting himself when the blood began to soak her clothes and the ground. He tried to wrap his shirt around her and tell her it was all right, for he thought she might be afraid or sorry. But she was neither, instead she held him as if she knew something he wouldn't know for years.

"I gave him lunch," Sarah told the porch people. "He sat with his legs straight out in front of him, so thin, they looked like bamboo shoots. His arms, too, and his hair sat so thick and wiry I thought it might be impossible to comb." Karl held his drink in his hands, between his legs, and he looked as if he had not heard what Sarah told, but might be thinking of something else. He smiled.

Karl was a man who had little time for humor, but he chose Sarah who did not share his seriousness. She provided a home where laughter and foolish ways were natural, but it took many years for Karl to learn. He held a strong German accent all his life and often felt accused or hated for his background. Sometimes he was right. As he grew older, he learned to tease with the children and whenever he did he knew Sarah had taught him that.

People on the porch stirred, someone getting ready to tell something of his own. A few had left already, one or two more wandered in. They were pleasant people, interested in the act of storytelling and listening. The children learned the art of storytelling from these groups, though not getting their own chance until they came of age. Boys and girls of fifteen or sixteen were allowed to venture something short, the grown-ups listening, not interfering. But if someone too young tried, they were cut off with "Be quiet now, honey. Listen," as though there had to be, needed to be, those required years of listening before one could venture to tell anything.

The day bed was full of children. Not one more could be fitted on it.

There was a sweet, oily smell of wild clematis, a heavy scent that settled on the porch and blew across everyone as the door opened. The scent was mixed with the smell of mild rubbish kept in cans that sat not too far away from the porch.

When the screen door slammed, it was J. B. Mott and everyone looked up. J.B. couldn't read, or write, but he ran the only bar in town, a quiet one; and he helped out sometimes at Locke's Store. People liked J.B. He was harmless enough, and he always had something interesting to tell, didn't come unless he had something. So, when he entered, all porch faces turned to him.

"What's happened, J.B.?" one face asked.

"They have it down there that somebody new just came in." He pointed toward the town.

"Who?"

"Some guy. A Doc. He has a boy with him. The boy's not

100

right in the head, I think. Don't act like it. He's retarded or something." J.B. moved over to the day bed and sat on the floor leaning against the children's row of feet. "Anyway, they came in yesterday."

"Where from?"

"Rossville, Georgia, I think he said. Yeah, it was Rossville. He's setting up practice here. I told him we already had a Doc, but he said he knew that and that he didn't want to change that none, just thought he could help out, relieve him some. So I told him maybe that'd be good."

People nodded.

"What about the boy?" One of the day bed voices ventured.

"He's about six or seven, I'd say. But he carries on like he's about three. The Doc took him into Locke's Store and gave him some candy. He ate it before Doc could even pay, then wanted another." The day bed giggled, the mothers said "Hm!" "And when Doc said no, that boy threw a fit. You've never seen such a thing. That Doc, he marched the boy out of the store so fast. He first talked, and tried to reason with the boy, then he just picked him up and carried him away." J.B. wiped his brow. "Whew! If he was one of *mine*!" J.B. had eight children, and was known to be a strict disciplinarian.

"Well," said one of the women. "That's a hard road for that man."

"He ain't married. I know that. He told me it was just him and the boy, and that he was the boy's uncle."

"Where'll they live?"

"Got an apartment. That old place next to the post office."

It was completely dark now. The day bed was settled, tired, no longer restless. Sarah offered to get ice cream for everybody, and some of the women went with her to dish it out in paper cups.

Karl received his ice cream, but continued to drink. The day bed ate voluptuously and wanted more. Sarah handed out sec-

101

onds before she had a chance to sit down with her own. "Now this is the last," she would say, but still get more. She had seemed very young to Karl on that day of their picnic—a southern girl raised in the shelter of nurses and black women and protective fathers and brothers. But as years went by, Karl found a strength and independence in this woman, and it was comparable to the force he saw in his grandmother the day they left Germany. And he leaned back into it as he would a big chair.

"What's their names?" The last question.

"Sam Parham. That's the doctor. The boy, I don't know his." J.B. took his cup of ice cream. No one even asked what kind, taking any kind offered. "But he's okay."

That was how Soldier and Sam Parham were introduced into the town. The porch people deciding they could stay, accepting them that night like a trial jury.

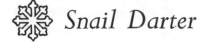 *Snail Darter*

In the middle of a hollowed-out room, a man leaned to remember being carried somewhere. Not carried on a horse. He didn't remember that. But he remembered being carried in someone's arms and then on a train, though at the time he didn't think of it as being a train. He only knew it now, when he was older and could stand at the train station, waiting. He didn't wait for anything or to go anywhere, but stood, then sat, looking up to the huge space above him. He loved the sooty smell. He loved to hear the steady clacking of wheels when the train came in, see the deep steamy burst of air when it stopped. And he thought of the man who brought him here.

His first trip on the train began one day in the spring forty-seven years ago. He was six and came to this town in Tennessee after recovering from an illness. His body had recovered sufficiently, but his mind stayed locked and he had the stare not of a regular six year old, but of someone who was bored or preoccupied.

He had had a fever. When his mother gave him laudanum to help him sleep, she forgot she gave the first dose and gave him a second. It was enough to put him into a deep, limp sleep that almost took him.

The doctor arrived to see the boy's stillness and ordered a horse to be saddled. He asked for three heavy belts. The mother did as she was told. Doctor Sam Parham was not the only

103

doctor in town, but he was the one everyone trusted the most. He placed the child in front of him on the horse and wrapped two of the large belts around them both, strapping the child to his own chest and waist. The child's head bent downward. They galloped off.

The mother, who had not asked anything until now, called after the doctor "Where are you going?," but they did not go anywhere. They rode back and forth in front of the farmhouse to jog the child awake. The doctor rode hard for hours and even when it began to rain he didn't stop, letting the rain sting their faces. The mother watched from the window. The father was not around.

They ran like that all night. The horse's mouth frothed, but the doctor would not stop or rest, nor did he allow the horse to rest. Toward the end, before morning, the horse's gallop turned measured and slow. So the doctor hit the horse with the other belt, on the high brown haunches, hitting and hitting, because the child had begun to stir, make noises, groans. But the horse was not able to give more running. The doctor's bladed belt pushed down the hooves into the soft earth, then raised them again, the effort giving the effect of speed. But the speed had slowed, so that the child was barely jogged now. When morning broke, the horse died.

And if someone had been watching (the mother at the window slumped asleep, her other children asleep), if someone had been there to see in those furious moments before morning, they would have felt the mindless life of the horse move into the boy, awaken him, giving only one way out of that black hollow where they had spent the night. And they would have heard the doctor shouting, and the horse's hooves steady against the slow earth, and above all, the labored breathing sounds.

The child had already opened his eyes, waking only slightly, never coming all the way back. The doctor carried the boy into the house, the boy as light as shadow. And the families who had given their children laudanum when they were sick no longer kept that medicine in their houses.

The doctor took the boy to live with him, appealing to the courts to allow it. The mother, a thin, furtive woman with a house full of children she couldn't care for, did not protest; but let it happen the way the doctor wanted. The day they left town, the boy carried a satchel as thin as paper, the other children played in the yard, and the mother stood with her back to them as she stirred something boiling on the stove. She waved with the flat of her hand, but the doctor knew when they drove off that she stood again at the window. When the child called for his mother, the doctor patted his knee or his shoulder or kept his hand on the boy's head. He told the child that he was his uncle, and over the years it was an easy lie for the boy to believe.

The spring day they arrived in Sweetwater, Tennessee, a downpour of rain caught them as they walked between the train and the station house. The boy, who loved the rain more than he loved the sunshine, said "Stand, stand," which meant he wanted to stand in the rain. The doctor urged him inside the station house with the promise of candy or a balloon. But he couldn't offer anything as fine as rain.

The doctor enrolled the boy in school and he was promoted through grades along with his age level. Each year the difference became more apparent. Children would ask him his name and when Oliver said "Oliver Brise," it came out garbled and sounded like "Abba." The children laughed and called him Abba all through grade school.

"Abba means 'father' in Hebrew," his uncle told him, trying to cheer him, give him pride in a name the children chose in cruelty. But Oliver liked the name and didn't feel the cruelty, not in that, at least. The cruelty Oliver bore was in the exclusion he felt.

105

"Abba. Abba has his pants on backwards," one boy yelled during the middle of a history lesson. They were in the ninth grade.

"Abba is fine." The teacher called him Abba too. She knew he had never worn his pants wrong, and the others knew too. The only one who doubted was Oliver who looked down to see if he had done everything right, zipped, buckled, everything. He was never sure.

He knew one girl, Edith Setler. She was not the prettiest girl in school, but she wasn't the ugliest either. Sometimes Edith walked him home, sometimes she sat beside him at lunch so that the other girls began to do the same. The boys started to invite Oliver to join their games. Oliver was never happier than in that ninth grade year. The next year he took a job and didn't see his friends except at the drugstore or around town where they still spoke to him and sometimes asked him to sit down. Oliver joined them, but he knew not to stay long.

The year Edith was a senior, Oliver saw her walking home from school and called to her. She stopped, stood for a moment, as though she couldn't think of his name. Then she said, "Oliver," and they walked along together. He had just taken a job as paperboy. Edith asked him about it.

"It's good." Oliver's head stiffened with the effort to sound normal.

"How's your uncle?"

"He's fine." He looked to the books Edith carried and frowned at the signs and symbols on one.

"Trigonometry," Edith told him. He tried to repeat the word but couldn't. "And it's sure not easy." She rolled her eyes in the way she used to, to indicate difficulty. Oliver laughed.

"Not easy," he said, and took hold of Edith's hand.

Oliver had grown to be six-feet-two-inches tall. He was not good-looking, but didn't have a distorted look. His eyes were particularly large and held that same blankness they had always had. "Edith," he said, not knowing what he would do next, not even knowing what he wanted to do, except that he had wanted for all those years to hold her hand. But now, as he did, a larger impulse swept over him and he pulled her against him, her books hitting against his chest and stomach and her head bumping his chin. She dropped her books and ran from him.

Oliver stood at the corner and saw her move away, her blue dress flying up around her knees and thighs, her arms moving out beside her as if for balance. When she turned and saw he was not chasing her, she stopped and stood for what seemed to Oliver a long while. Then she called to him. Oliver didn't answer. He stooped to pick up her books and looked up once to see if she still stood there. His face was red with an embarrassment he didn't understand. A storekeeper saw the incident and came out, but saw Oliver picking up the books and didn't see anything wrong. Others stood at the windows of shops to watch what Edith would do. She returned to where Oliver was. He handed her books to her, her papers stacked neatly on top.

Before Edith took the books she put her hand on his shoulder, and Oliver's mind went suddenly to the loss of his mother that day and the doctor's touch on his shoulder and knee and head. He felt comforted.

"I'm sorry," said Edith. Oliver nodded and said it was okay. She took the books from him, and told him she'd see him tomorrow.

Oliver continued down the street in the same direction as Edith, knowing that he had moved from a confusion that felt devastating to a confusion that felt good. Edith's blue dress swished as she walked and he showed his gratefulness to her from that time on by merely waving to her from far off. But sometimes when he passed her house, she might come out and they would talk and she would ask how he was.

* * *

107

Oliver couldn't remember the name of the town he was born in. He only knew that Sweetwater was his home, though sometimes he made trips to other towns with his uncle. He knew that this man was his uncle. He knew too, though vaguely, of a ride long ago on a horse and how the horse died as Oliver himself had lived through that night. The spurious courage of that night and of the doctor's decision to take him away from his home. Oliver had been told the story, so that his remembering came more from the telling than from memory. And each time he was told, he knew that the horse's death meant both his own life and his own doom, though he couldn't say how he knew this. And he knew that moving to Sweetwater with his uncle had somehow saved his life.

One year before his uncle died, there was an uproar around Tennessee which involved the building of the Tellico Dam and a small fish, two-and-one-half-inches long, called the snail darter. The dam's configuration blocked the fish from reaching the spawning grounds upstream, and unless they were relocated the chance of their becoming extinct was almost assured. It was thought at that time that Sweetwater, Tennessee, was the only place left where the snail darter could survive, and the building of the dam was stopped by order of the Supreme Court. Oliver's uncle followed the story and told it to Oliver, who loved the idea that people would stop the building of the dam to find a new home for the fish. Biologists came to Tennessee to designate a seventeen-mile stretch of shallow water as a Critical Habitat. But at the same time, there were bands of Cherokee Indians who were also affected by the building of the dam. The water would flood more than twenty of their sacred villages including the village of Tanasi, which had become the name of the state. The doctor crusaded for both the Indians and the snail darter and found an irony in the attention given to the two-and-one-half-inch fish.

Everyone talked about the snail darter and how it stopped

108

the building of the Tellico Dam and the doctor liked to tell Oliver how they, too, had been relocated, brought to Sweetwater, the water they would live in.

When Sam Parham left Rossville, Georgia, he wanted to go anywhere. Sweetwater happened to be the place he chose. He had fallen in love with a married woman in Rossville. She returned his affection, but then one day ran off with a man Sam had never seen nor heard of. Sam was, by then, thirty-seven years old. He had lost hope of having a wife and children and settled into his idea of bachelorhood and reclusiveness with determination, but not much happiness.

The day he saw the boy, Oliver, an instinct rose in him that could not be called anything but paternal. As the boy recovered, the instinct increased, and the doctor grew to love him. He felt two things: that if he lost this part of himself that was able to care for the boy, he might lose his capacity to love anyone, and more important, there was the danger that the mother might again give the boy an overdose. He appealed to the court, saying that the boy was brain-damaged and as a doctor he could give better care as it was needed. Since the mother didn't protest, but remained wordless, agreeing to the court with nods and shrugs, the court gave the boy to the doctor.

But from the beginning the doctor saw how difficult it would be to take care of the child, so he hired a housekeeper, someone to be with Oliver when the doctor wasn't home. The woman he found had been a nurse and though she didn't mention why she was no longer in that profession, she seemed capable enough. He hired her.

Oliver was almost seven when Mrs. Constant came to work for them. She had no trouble with the boy and was able even to control him when he flew into one of his tantrums.

109

"Constant," he yelled, "bring Abba a comb." But Mrs. Constant would not do everything Oliver wanted.

"You can get the comb yourself, Oliver dear," she would say and after a stubborn silent refusal or else a demanding Indianlike yell, Oliver got up to get the comb himself. Sometimes he threw it at her, sometimes he combed his hair in front of the mirror then messed it up with his hands, pulling it straight up so that he looked as if he were floating underwater. Mrs. Constant would take the comb and fix his hair, neatly parting and smoothing down the sides. She ignored him when he ran his fingers through it to undo what she had done. The doctor praised her patience, her ability to hold her temper.

Once when Oliver threw the comb, he was standing very close to Mrs. Constant, so that the comb hit hard on the side of her nose. She reached and slapped his cheek, and though this did not surprise Oliver, the doctor had to leave the room to keep from interfering. He noted the next day that there was still a faint patch of red on the boy's cheek, but the boy seemed to have forgotten.

The way Oliver remembered that block of time—the year or two when he stayed his nonschool hours with Mrs. Constant —was this: he remembered her large body which seemed to him like some huge rock, and he remembered when she had to stay with him at night because the doctor would be gone. He remembered how she screamed at him when he couldn't sleep, or if he woke with a nightmare and called out. He could still see, sometimes at night, her big, stocky, fat-legged figure bursting into his room, so that he knew he must have cried out or made some noise or shout that brought her, because she came at him, appearing suddenly. And she seemed to be in flight, a huge bird that hung over him. He could even hear from her small birdlike sounds that came not from her mouth but from her throat as she filled the night with her consternations. And it seemed to Oliver at those times that there were more people there, more than just this bird woman who descended and hovered above him whenever he cried out and woke her from sleep.

"I'll teach you," she cried. Her voice had the quality of a hissing goose. "You broke my sleep." Her red hair flew in all directions, her breath rank with a smell Oliver couldn't identify. She hit Oliver. Her fists, at first, lay closed and hard against his head, then her fingers opened to scratch him, make him bleed. Sometimes she lifted something from the floor and used it. If the thing she chose was heavy, Oliver would be knocked unconscious. Oliver didn't know why she came in to him during those nights, but thought, as children do, that it was surely his fault and that he would be glad when the hitting stopped as it always did.

Oliver's mind wanted only to fall asleep, quiet and sleep. When she left and he watched her go back down the hallway, a lassitude settled on him, made him unable even to cover himself. Rarely did she come back twice in one night. Some nights, though, she would not come in at all and when Oliver woke and saw the dawn he knew he had slept through and had not suffered her hands. And he always believed on those mornings that these terrible nights were over.

It was a January night that it ended. His uncle arrived home earlier than expected. Oliver heard the car drive up and tried to mention it to Mrs. Constant.

"Constant. Constant."

But Constant yelled her drunken talk, saying much that made no sense to anyone but herself. And Oliver was always surprised how the next morning she would be sitting at the kitchen table with toast and jelly, offering to fix eggs any way he wanted. But at night all he saw was her stoutness coming toward him against the hall light. Her fists ready.

His uncle was in the room by the time she had hit him twice. He threw her against the far wall, startling her into a fit of short rage, then crying, then pleading.

Oliver watched dumbly. He watched his uncle, or the man

111

he now called his uncle, yell at this woman to get out, get *out*, *get out*. His face raged in the same way hers had, only this time not at him. Oliver, relieved to have the protection, had not expected it or even thought to ask for it.

Constant left. They never saw her again. The doctor looked over Oliver's body to find bruises, cuts the woman had made. Some of them were already healed. He stayed near the boy until sunup, not sleeping, but staying to cradle Oliver. The boy slept, though fitfully. And when he woke with his inevitable nightmares, the doctor was there to say, "It's okay. Okay, Oliver," saying it over and over again, like a cant. "Go back to sleep. I'm here. I'm here." And he would brush the boy's hair from his forehead with one hand.

It was past sunup when the doctor himself went to sleep.

There was a space of about ten years when Oliver wore a blue serge suit. He wore it both summer and winter, though in winter he wore a heavy coat over it. The suit grew shiny and people began to mention to his uncle that he should have a new one. But Oliver didn't want new clothes. Finally, someone gave him a soldier's coat, medals still on it, captain's bars intact. They gave him two pair of gray pants to go with it. For a while Oliver wore only the pants and the jacket he had worn before. But his uncle saw him try on the coat in front of the long hall mirror, walking back and forth, saluting. Then one day he wore it into town. He saluted everyone, making the gesture a little high with fingers pointing upward as the British do. No one corrected him, but returned the salute and began to call him Soldier. He liked the name.

Soldier ran all his years in Sweetwater, ran as smooth as he could. He took jobs his uncle found for him and when his uncle died, he took from the town. Now his face grows rounded and more aged, not aging as quickly as his body. His eyes stay young, though, and so does the way he walks or rides his bike.

Some days he sits at the train station, and watches the one train come and go. He sits on the steps of the trains parked in their stalls, but mostly he sits inside the station house. People think he remembers his early train ride and that that longing brings him here, but he isn't reminded of anything exactly, he only returns to sit at a familiar place.

But there are moments when he seems to remember, when his body moves into a position. He turns his head as though he has heard something and just been caught in a snapshot. And at those times, when he listens, gives all his attention, his back sits straight, not slumped. He is a picture already taken, his head held with an abrupt dignity, like that of a servant who feels proud in his work.

But all the while something works inside him. He sees his mother at the stove, lifting only the flat of her hand when he left, and Soldier holds his two hands together.

He spends his life marveling (without knowing he has marveled) at what he has lost. He wonders where his life is, feeling at some point it was shifted. He wants to be carried somewhere. So he leans into the dark smell of the station house and finds comfort in the high-ceilinged room, the black glint of long narrow track. He finds comfort in strangers who speak or nod. But he could no more say what that comfort was than he could say what makes him feel lonely or tired.

Sometimes he says out loud, not to anyone, but out loud, "Please, don't make me remember that."

Mama, I Cut My Hand

Ty ran off the day after the circus. No one knew until later. Jacob saw him at the schoolhouse, but Ty didn't come home at four o'clock, and by suppertime he still wasn't home.

He went to Callie's house. He had been there before with his friends, had peeked through Callie's windows, but Callie hadn't seen them. So when Ty ran off, he went there, not knowing he would go there, just deciding late in the day. He walked to the edge of town and wondered how far it was to Murfreesboro. He had been there once with his mother, but couldn't remember how long it took to get there. It occurred to him that it had taken a long time, so he turned instead toward the caves and toward Callie's house in the woods. As he walked, his mind settled into the idea that he might live with Callie for several years before anyone found him.

Upon approaching her gray, unsettled porch, he wished for his friends to be with him and suddenly hated the thought of running away by himself. He knocked on Callie's door and waited so long for her to answer that he finally sat down on the porch steps, getting up once to knock again, hearing Callie inside moving around but not coming to the door. He finally called to her, saying her name, Callie, because he didn't know anything else to call her. And when she opened the door, it was as though she didn't recognize him, but was glad to see him anyway. And she said, as she talked to him, "Jacob. Come over here, honey," and Ty came but didn't correct her, though once he said, "My name's Ty," and Callie looked at him, smiled. She said, "Ty," as though she wasn't sure if that was a name or what. Then the next time she said something she would again call him Jacob. She touched his shoulders and back in a way that he liked.

Jacob felt sure the reason Ty ran off lay in their excursion to the circus. The newspaper wrote up the incident, but didn't make it sound as horrifying as it really was, saying how the elephant posed a danger to hundreds of people and in order to prevent an accident or someone else being killed, they had to destroy the animal. It was that simple. Jacob mentioned to Verna that he was sorry about the circus.

"That's not it," Verna told Jacob. She held the baby. "Not that." Verna called the police. They searched for Ty, though no one thought of Callie's house.

When Ty was found (and he was found when he himself decided to go home, being finally bored at Callie's), he was found heading toward his house. The policeman swooped him up and carried him to Verna as though he had performed a rescue. Ty was gone long enough that Verna did not show anger, but felt grateful to see him; though after a few minutes, she began to reprimand and threaten punishment, not this time, but if he ever did it again. Then she showed again her gratefulness.

Ty exhibited to his mother a small cut that was bothering him, and he even began to cry about it so that Verna gave the cut her attention, wondering if it might be deeper than it looked.

Cedar, who had been alternately worried and envious of the episode, told Ty she wanted her balloon back. Ty said he lost it. (It was at Callie's.) Then Cedar said, "Why did you run off?"

Ty said he didn't know. He looked again to his cut, wishing

115

for more attention to be paid to it and less to him. Jacob went to get a Band-Aid for it.

Then Verna walked to the next room to answer the baby's cries, to bring it in, cradle it, letting all the attention now refocus on the new brother. So Ty began to scream that Jacob had wrapped the Band-Aid too tight and that it was hurting, a pain unbearable, and his crying grew into sobs until Jacob loosened the Band-Aid, then took the new baby from Verna so that she could soothe Ty.

"Oh, Mama, I cut my hand." His sobs were even harder now.

"Let's see, honey. Let's see."

And Jacob saw that Verna had been right—that to Ty, what he had seen the night before was not as horrible as the replacement he felt by his brother. Not even the elephant still smoldering next to the woods, next to the stobs where the circus tent had been bolted down.

Ty went to Cedar's room that night. He had come to her room before at night, but it had been several years since he had done so.

"Cedar?" He wanted to see if she was awake, or to wake her.

"Huh?"

"I want to tell you something."

"What?" Cedar sat up.

"When I went off," he sat in a chair opposite her bed. Cedar was sitting and looking to the end of the bed, so that they were lined up with each other. "I went to Callie's house."

"Callie's? She let you in?"

"Yeah."

"You been there before?" Cedar guessed.

"Yeah."

Cedar waited a moment. "You scared everybody. Nobody knew what happened."

Ty was silent.

116

"We didn't know," said Cedar, thinking he didn't understand or hear. "What was it like, Callie's house?"

"A house." He waited a minute. "She was nice though. She gave me some things to eat."

"Like what?"

"Like some soup." Ty hated soup. "It was good." He waited some more. "You know when Jonathan fell into the ice? That day?"

Cedar nodded.

"I ran home and told Mama."

"I know," said Cedar. "I ran home with you. I told her too." She could not understand why he didn't remember her presence with him on that day, but talked as if he had been there alone. "I was there too," she said.

"And now Joseph."

"What?" said Cedar.

"I wish he wasn't here."

"He's all right," said Cedar. "Come here. I'll show you." She took Ty's hand and led him to the room next to her mother's where Joseph lay. He slept but was restless. "See?"

Ty didn't know what Cedar wanted him to see, but looked anyway. Joseph was ugly in the ways that babies that young are usually ugly, his face wrinkled, his hair black and long in sprouts along his neck. His eyes opened suddenly and fastened onto Ty so quickly that Ty jumped a little, feeling intrusive to be watching somebody asleep.

"Uh-oh. He's awake."

But Joseph didn't cry out, as if in league already with his brother and sister, not telling on them for being up so late. He closed his eyes again and rested, more heavily now.

"See?" said Cedar.

Ty reached into the crib to pull a corner of the cover away from Joseph's mouth and to straighten another part. Cedar left first. Ty went to bed after several more minutes.

The next day Ty offered to take Joseph for a walk in his

117

buggy. Verna let him, and it became an afternoon ritual—Ty taking Joseph out, both of them looking forward to it, both coming back with a sense of pride and uncommon accomplishment.

 # Small Ravenous Bird

From the window Callie could see the forest and beyond to the clearing. It was not yet dark, so the clearing beyond the forest was still bathed in the light that was left. Callie could see well enough to notice how the light changed during the day. She could tell the time of day by the way the light fell, and could judge within an hour even on cloudy days. She could see well enough to know if anyone approached, though hardly anyone did.

She knew now that Jacob was in town. Sophie told her, and Annie had come by in the afternoon, yesterday (or was it a week ago?) and told her. The information took a few moments to register on Callie's face.

He will come by here, I'm sure, Annie told her.

Soon. Tell him soon.

I will.

Callie knew of the deer hunt, or rather she remembered it from when Ruben used to go, and assumed it was a ritual the men continued.

They leave for Singer Woods on Sunday, Annie said.

Tell him to come before Sunday.

I will. Annie looked around. *You need anything?* Callie needed everything.

No.

I will tell him.

Annie saw herself to the door.

119

Callie waited at the window the rest of that day, and the next.

People came from all over the county for the dance held to bring in the first deer hunt. It was the women's idea. The men would be gone for a week, maybe two. The women billed it as a send-off, a celebration, though they all said they'd be lonely. The men felt foolish, but went along with it. The dance usually had some Indian theme, with a huge headdress made out of colored cups and toilet paper taped to the walls.

This year, instead of having the dance in the old barn, they held it in the largest room of a cave outside Sweetwater. The cave was a tourist attraction, and had several large chambers, one of which was called the Lost Sea and had a body of water the size of a lake, big enough for boats. The chamber used for the dance celebration was called the Great Hall. A few years ago, the town housed an evangelical meeting there, and since then they used it for everything. But when the dance moved to the cave the Indian theme dissolved, which seemed peculiar since the Indians had used this cave. There were artifacts showing evidence of the Cherokee.

Two hundred families came to the dance. A band was brought in from Knoxville. Old danced with young, middle-aged danced with old and young, teenagers danced only with other teenagers. Annie and Albert were there.

Jacob watched Annie tuck up loose strands of her hair from her neck. She stood in a way that made men watch her for a moment. At sixteen, Annie had a buxom figure, that as she grew older turned fat, but at sixteen made boys and men alike stare. Still, she gained attention, here, with most of them old; and she gave to them, even her brother, a moment's pleasure.

When the music began, Annie looked around for a partner. Jacob led her onto the dance floor, a wooden platform built for speakers or for bands, but the band had set up on the floor of the cave, and the people used the platform. It rumbled with

120

the weight of feet, and the energy in the Great Hall was that of a row of wild turkeys about to be shot. The men felt handsome and dangerous; the women felt admired, their desires candid and expectant. There was a power of mischief.

When the music stopped, everyone wanted more, so the band played another chorus of that song until everyone finished tired. Jacob and Annie moved toward the table of food. Annie said that Callie usually came to these dances and that she had expected to see her because her house was so close by.

"But she's not here," said Annie, "and I wonder if something's wrong."

Jacob didn't say anything. He didn't want to see Callie tonight.

"Maybe you could take her a plate of food," Annie urged. Jacob hated her for it.

He took the plate Annie handed him. She piled rolls on top, then wrapped it in a napkin.

"You mean *now*?" Jacob asked, his expression one of a little boy who is being made to do a chore he has put off all day and wants to put off longer.

"Well, maybe she'll want to come back here with you," Annie told him. "But it would be nice, even if she doesn't come, for somebody to take her the food."

It was easy to find where the path into the woods began. Jacob went straight into it. The music from the dance got farther and farther behind him. Had two weeks gone by already? Jacob had arrived the last of October and now it was well into November. He tried to look forward to seeing Callie.

But it wasn't Callie he was thinking of as he walked through the woods. For days now as he spoke with people (met them for the first time or renewed old acquaintances), it was as though his heart pressed heavy against his ribs, and there were times when his head felt asleep. He had been thinking of Drue, not in a conscious way, but the way that Drue had entered his thoughts for years, remembering some childhood scene in

121

which they were both included, or seeing himself with an awkward clarity running down the hill toward his car, seeing Drue's mask-emblem face.

Upon reaching the porch, he tripped on the steps. The plate of food did not spill. And Jacob, as he stood, resembled a man washed upon a beach, someone who had been swimming for many miles but now was back and too tired to think about anything.

This is what Callie saw from the window:

It was almost dark and she was not able to see his features, but she knew the shape of his head (the same as when a boy), and she knew his walk. She knew too he was carrying something and that he was coming to see her. The moment she saw him a warm trickle flowed down both her legs and she hurried to change her clothes.

He knocked twice, then came in, put the plate of food in the kitchen, and called to her. She hurried more, slipping her feet into her gardening shoes. She hoped the length of her dress might cover them.

"Callie?" he called. "Callie?"

Callie didn't answer. She didn't know why. She wanted him to find her. She placed a hat on her head and peeked out from behind the tall wood-framed mirror. She hoped she looked all right. But when she saw Jacob, she forgot how she looked and made a quick approach, or what she thought was a quick approach. She laid her head on his chest, resting both cheek and ear on his shirt. He was saying something. She pulled back. "Sit down," she told him.

The light in the room was like a light from several lanterns. There were a few small lamps turned on, but the fire in the huge fireplace made the room flicker with yellow light. The house itself smelled damp and slightly of soiled rags.

He had heard her in a room to his left, so he said "Callie?" then her large hat peeked out from behind the floor-length mirror and Jacob could see her feet. She wore a man's heavy brown brogans that were untied and halfway unlaced. He could see too, the hem of her long dress. He was only a few feet away, but called louder, thinking she might be deaf. "It's Jacob," he said, "Jake," and the brogans stepped out from behind the long mirror.

Her eyes were full of death. Death had hold on her, the way death takes hold of an old hound, not completely, but with a hard grip, so that he is slower and groans a bit when he walks. And maybe that hound came by years ago and hung around so that you fed him and still after fifteen years he's around, but nobody can even guess how old he is. And all the children who played with him have grown and left home, but when they come back he nudges them and they don't have much to say. That is the way Callie looked, as though what she saw was not from this world, but other-worldly. But that hound, he likes to go for walks, slow as he is, and sometimes, remembering, he chases a squirrel. Callie took another step toward Jacob.

Her dress hung to her ankles and was trimmed at the neck and wrists with lace. Another strip of lace lay tacked to her waist, but this piece drooped as though it had been added on later. Callie waved her arms, seeming to shoo him away or warn. She looked like someone who knows she is diseased and wants to wave away those she loves for fear of contaminating them. Jacob took one step back before he realized her waving was merely the excitement of pleasure. She held out a handkerchief, extending it to Jacob as she might to a child who needed to blow his nose. So he moved toward her with one large step and caught her. She felt like a bag of sticks.

When he let her go, she said, "Sit down," and stood before him, small, her head bowed. Her hat fell to the floor, and Jacob could see her scant hair. Her odor was that of the house, only stronger.

Jacob took the handkerchief. He thanked her for it. Her

123

face was as old as the world, older, a mirror in which he saw himself. He could not turn away from her, from the firelight that licked at her cheeks and seemed to make them wrinkle before his eyes, each time flooding a place that seemed drier and more creased than another place. He sat down and she offered him tea. When she turned away, Jacob noticed that the back of her dress had a line of buttons all the way down the spine. He was curious as to how she had buttoned them herself; but gaps of material lay open in the middle of her back and he knew her fingers had fumbled there.

"You wrote to me," said Jacob.

"Yes." But he wasn't sure she remembered.

"You asked me to come back."

"Yes."

"Something to tell me."

She seated herself and held the cup of tea chest-high, lifting it to her dry lips that pursed to sip. Jacob waited, not drinking his own tea.

"Is it all right?" Callie asked, indicating his cup steaming on the table.

Jacob lifted it and drank.

"I'm going to die," she told him, without any evidence of sadness or self-pity. Jacob found her directness made him want to smile. He didn't comment, but let her proceed. "And before I do, I want to say something to you about the night of Drue's burning."

Jacob guessed that was the way the town referred to it: Drue's burning. His chest tightened against his ribs and he heard again the revolver's sound.

"Drue was shot that night," she told Jacob. Still he said nothing.

What was she saying to him? Jacob saw Ty's balloon in the corner. It was small now, small as a tennis ball.

"I saw the flames from my house and got over there before the fire department."

124

Jacob remembered hearing the sirens of the fire engines. Callie must have called them, and she must have arrived only a little before Jacob himself had left.

What? His head was swimming.

"And I saw you," she told him, "going to your car."

Running. Running.

"And you were running. I called to you, but you didn't hear." Callie had taken only that one sip of her tea. Jacob had finished his.

"No," he said. He wished he had more tea.

"I saw you leave." Callie didn't say this in judgment. "Then I went into the hallway. I pulled Drue out."

Callie pulled Drue out.

"I wrapped the body with a rug and pulled him out best I could." Her voice was strong telling this, her head as clear as any mountain stream. Her sentences were spoken with complete clarity, so that Jacob felt their minds had switched and he had been given the confused, flustered state of someone close to a hundred years old.

"While I was doing that, a boy came around the corner of the house. He had been in the back, in the woods, I guess."

"Who?" Jacob found his voice.

"It was the boy who shot Drue. So young. Just a boy. He was twelve years old. He was crying, but he never told. There were three of us who knew and decided to keep the matter quiet. For the boy," she said.

"Who?" Jacob could not ask more, could not think of anything else to ask; but he remembered now in the back window that had reflected the yellow firelight, the faint image of a young boy's face, looking in, wide-eyed, frightened. He remembered that face though he had never really thought of it. "Who was it?" he asked.

But Callie waved him off. "You will know," she told him, "because he will talk to you. I only wanted to prepare you in some way." Then she said, "I have never told his name." Callie

125

said this last with a pride, a loyalty she was proud of, wishing, Jacob thought, that someone had done the same for her.

"No one ever mentioned this," Jacob said.

"After I wrapped Drue in the rug, the firemen came. They were busy trying to save the house. I said I would sit with Drue until the doctor got there. I told the boy to go home and not to tell anyone." Callie shifted her position. "I wasn't sure what that boy would do, because he came around the house crying, saying how he had done it. I told him not to worry, that we would take care of it, and to go on home. It was late, anyway, about nine thirty by then."

"And he went home?"

She nodded. "Then Doc and me went to Judge Bradford. Told him. And the Judge agreed how we should keep it away from the newspaper. The Doc took complete care of Drue, doing an autopsy and repairing whatever needed to be repaired before they gave him to be buried. The Doc saw to all of that." Callie's voice was firm and strong. "Then he announced how death had been caused by severe burns and smoke inhalation. The Judge confirmed it, and since I found the body and pulled it out, I confirmed it too."

Jacob's head nodded like a puppet's.

"We didn't want to ruin that boy's life," Callie said. She knew how that could happen. "He's turned out fine, so I believe we did the right thing."

Jacob stood and walked across the room away from Callie. *It's impossible*, Jacob thought, *that Callie held this from me all these years. How could she never mention it?* so he asked her.

"How could you not say anything to me all these years?" Jacob's voice sounded different. "Not tell me what happened?"

Callie's face looked as if she thought that this telling had backfired, that instead of doing her the good she hoped it might do to speak to Jacob, there was the possibility of setting him against her. He was the only person she felt still loved her. "What do you mean?" she asked him.

126

For once in his life, Jacob didn't know if Callie was telling him the truth. Her voice grew low, her head bent down, but Jacob couldn't feel any sympathy for her.

"How could you let me believe all this time that *I* had been the reason for Drue's death?"

"Oh, Jake," Callie stood and approached Jacob, shaky, wobbly, from standing too quickly. The one hundred years entering her again.

"I left him there," Jacob said.

"I know, I know." Then she stopped a moment, remembering something. "Jake?" She faced him. "You *saw* Drue? I mean, when he fell you could see how he was?" She meant the hole in Drue's chest that she had covered with the rug.

Jacob nodded. "And I heard the gun." He waited before he said, "And I wondered if *I* had done it."

"I knew there was something, but I didn't know what." The firelight licked against her and she whispered, "Jake, I swear to you," but she didn't know what to swear. "I could never mention Drue's name, because whenever I did your expression would change. Something in you would turn away. And even now," she told him, "as we talk about it now, both of us knowing everything. . . ."

"Not everything," Jacob said. "There was more. Earlier." But he said it low so she couldn't hear.

Callie stood directly in front of Jacob inclining her head to him. And though Jacob was taller, much taller, he held his hands lightly behind his back. So it seemed as though Callie were a strict teacher who had asked him to recite and even though Jacob had studied and practiced his lessons, he could not remember, could say nothing.

"Jacob, that boy wants to talk to you," Callie said, "but I thought I should talk to you first. Tell you what I know." Jacob had never seen anyone so sad as she said, "I hope I've done the right thing."

Callie's voice provided for Jacob the magical effect against

127

his neck and shoulder blades, but somehow he wanted more. He knew that she meant for him to feel relief. All she had done was to protect one boy's life from being what her own life had been. The light from the lamp was not a light to see by, but merely sprayed the room, hitting above and below the lampshade, hitting the table and floor and ceiling, but not doing anything to illuminate the room. Callie waited for Jacob to speak. Her face expected something from him, so he forced into his expression a calmness. He had no idea what he looked like, but felt foolish as though maybe his expression was contorted. But his look, whatever it was, seemed to satisfy.

He told her Of course, she had done the right thing, and when he said it Callie pulled him to her, a quick bony gesture that took hold of him the way you imagine death might do. And when she did, the room to Jacob grew suddenly damp, so that he felt chilled. And a shudder went quickly through him like a rolling egg.

When Jacob left Callie's house, he had been there almost an hour.

"Will you be back?" Callie asked, and her demeanor had changed from strength to weakness, but only a physical weakness.

"Yes." He meant it.

Jacob had placed the plate of food on the kitchen table. He hoped she would find it. "The food I brought's in the kitchen," he said. But again, he wasn't sure if she heard.

They walked onto the porch and Callie put her arm around Jacob's waist. They didn't face each other, but looked into the woods. It was too dark to see anything, but still they looked.

"You'll be back?" she asked again. It was not an answer she wanted from him, but a reassurance of making plans that could help her believe her life would go on.

Then she turned quickly to put her arms around him, and pressed her palms firmly onto his back. She didn't pull him to her as though she needed anything from him. She didn't ask him to stay, but her look was so bold with affection that Jacob wondered if it took nearly a century to learn to hold someone this way.

"Yes."

Jacob turned around once after he left the porch, told her "Go on in now. You might chill." He hoped she would eat the food while it was hot, but her needs now no longer seemed physical, or else nothing physical could fill them. He saw from the woods, the firelight behind her. She could not see him, but called out anyway. Words of caution: "It's so dark, Jake. Careful, now." She reminded him of a bird: her thinness, her light, uncertain, hopping kind of walk. Her glad heart. Her voice sounded thin too, though the sound was pure and called to him like a wren or some other small ravenous bird.

A Large Sturdy Face

When Jacob returned to the dance, he waved to Annie to let her know everything was okay, but noticed a commotion over near the punch table. Two men talked loudly, wanting the attention of everyone, though they spoke only to Soldier. Their voices carried as if they were actors in a play.

"Tell us the joke about the woman and the dog," said the older man. His voice was falsely good-natured.

"I don't remember."

"Sure you do."

Jacob did not walk over to them, but watched. He thought maybe they were showing kindness with their urgings.

"Sure you do," repeated the younger man (who was not young, but younger by ten years than the man beside him). And he pushed Soldier slightly in the chest with two fingers. "Tell the story about the woman and the dog."

"What are they *doing*?" Jacob asked Annie as she walked over to him.

"How is Callie? Did you take her the food?"

"Yes. What are they *doing*?"

They both turned again to watch.

Soldier was the town's paperboy and had done that job now for years. The people in town usually tolerated his jokes and stories, but these men taunted him. Jacob didn't know why.

"Here," said the youngest man. "Here. Drink this down."

130

"I don't want it," said Soldier, visibly upset. He wouldn't look at either man, but looked down at the table and the punch bowl. He wrung his hands with nervous energy. It was the only time Jacob had ever seen anyone actually wring their hands. "I have to go," Soldier finally said.

The older man took the glass of punch with whiskey in it and said, "We offered this to you nice now, so why don't you just stay a minute and talk to us."

Soldier looked around to see if anyone watched. Many watched, but did not interfere. No one knew if these men were teasing Soldier in a regular way or in a way that they should step in and interfere. Since no one wanted to appear foolish, they waited.

"Well, for just a minute," Soldier gave in to the pressure that the older man applied to his arm, and settled again into a straight-backed chair where he had been sitting. The two men sat down too, smiling. Soldier still wrung his hands.

Sophie called over to the two men. She was bringing out more punch for the punch bowl. "You leave him alone now. You know he can't drink that." But her words came out more as duty than as forceful authority. And when Jacob looked at her, he thought she had the look of someone who was enjoying the show. Her hair was dyed blacker for this night.

Then Sophie walked over to explain to Jacob. "He's allergic to anything alcoholic. Makes him break out in large welts for days. He's the strangest thing you've ever seen when he does that."

"Do they *make* him drink it?"

"Sometimes." She wished to ease Jacob's expression, so she said, "Oh, it's all right. He doesn't mind. He *enjoys* the attention since his uncle died. Actually, I think he likes it."

Jacob turned to see how Soldier liked it. The men threatened to pour the punch on his leg and Soldier squirmed as though he thought it might have the effect of acid.

131

"I'll tell the one about the woman and the dog," he said finally, his eyes blank and inscrutable. Sophie smiled at the situation the way an adult smiles when a young child cries over something that doesn't matter, the adult knowing the sadness won't last.

"Tell us," the younger man said and handed the drink to Soldier.

By this time Jacob had walked to where Soldier sat. He lifted the punch from Soldier's hand and threw it onto the young man's shirt, a quick, impulsive splash that seemed like a slap. There was silence in the Great Hall, people not knowing whether to laugh.

The man looked to his shirt as though he thought he had spilled it himself, not quite believing Jacob had done it. Jacob said, "Soldier," and his voice boomed as loud as the playactors, "Did you want to hit this man?" And Jacob was about to repeat his words, thinking that Soldier needed to be urged, but as he started to repeat, he saw Soldier's arm draw into the air, his hand making a fist the size of a softball. And he raised it high to let it come down flat on top of the younger man's head. The man had stood up, but his knees buckled slightly as though the force were the force of a heavy mallet. Then Soldier used his other fist to hit the man's stomach, knocking out his breath and bending him low into a formal bow.

People clapped, changing their allegiance to whomever was giving the most pleasure. Jacob led Soldier to the benches lining the walls. Sophie brought a rag to let him wipe his face, because his fear had caused him to drool.

"How often does this go on?" Jacob asked. Soldier did not answer, but seemed concerned now with the rag and with Sophie wiping his face. "Why do they do it?" Jacob turned to get his answer from Annie. Annie didn't know what to answer, so she looked back to Soldier. His face broke into a huge smile as he bit into a sandwich from a plate beside him.

132

"I know a joke," he told them. "Want to hear?"

Sophie said she wanted to hear. Jacob stared at Soldier's mouth, a little open and stupid. His hair was gray.

The two men, still at the punch bowl, decided to leave. The older man's face held a look of severe disgust, but no one knew if he was disgusted with Soldier or with Jacob or with the young man who walked out now beside him, bending over.

Cedar and Ty ran to Jacob, proud. Cedar asked him to dance. They danced three dances in a row.

When the dance was over, Annie offered to drive Soldier home; and though Soldier walked it often, he could not resist the chance for a car ride. He sat in the back with Jacob.

The apartment house where Soldier lived was an old one. He lived on the top floor. The landlord let him stay after his uncle died.

Soldier tripped slightly on the curb as he got out, but caught himself and did not fall completely down. Jacob said he would go upstairs with him, and followed Soldier to his two-room apartment. It was neat and clean and had the evidence of someone compulsive about order. Some newspapers were stacked almost to the ceiling.

"Sometimes people call," Soldier explained, "and they tell me not to deliver their papers for a week, so I don't." He placed his soldier's coat on the bed. "But then they call back and they're mad." He looked as though he were trying to figure out a puzzle. "They fuss at me because they had to pay when the papers were not delivered."

"That's because," said Jacob, and his voice took on a tone of infinite patience, "they want you to tell the newspaper not to bill them."

Soldier looked at his stack of papers in the corner as though he wondered what good it would do to tell those newspapers anything. "That's stupid," he told Jacob.

And Jacob said he guessed it was, at that.

133

Soldier offered to make some coffee, but Jacob reminded him that Annie and Albert waited in the car.

"I forgot," said Soldier and it was the first sign of embarrassment Jacob had seen in him.

"I did too," said Jacob, acting as though he must hurry to make up for his own forgetting. He was almost down the second flight of stairs when he heard Soldier call to him, and he looked up to see a big face bent over the dark wood banister.

"Jacob," Soldier yelled. It was the first time he had called Jacob by name. "You brought me home, and you helped me," he was explaining something. He mentioned that he wanted to take Jacob somewhere, but his speech was garbled and Jacob was not yet used to understanding all that he said.

"What, Soldier?"

"The Lost Sea," Soldier explained, speaking more slowly. "I work there." Soldier had another job in the chamber of the cave where people could go in boats.

"And you take people in the boats?" Jacob helped him explain. "On the Lost Sea?"

"Yes." Soldier nodded vigorously. He straightened to think, then bent down over the banister again almost immediately. He bent so far that Jacob hoped he wouldn't fall. "I could take you in my boat," Soldier said and it seemed to be an effort to repay.

"That'd be fine." Jacob wondered when they would go, or if Soldier would forget. He continued down the flight of stairs thinking that maybe Cedar and Ty could go too. He was on the ground floor when he heard Soldier call good-bye.

Jacob waved and looked up through the stairwell before going out. He could see Soldier still bending over to watch him. The light from the high ceiling shone above, and his large sturdy face hung there, bold as a planet.

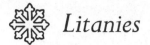 *Litanies*

Tom had called and left the message that he would not come for the hunting trip after all, but would be in Virginia for Christmas. Jacob knew he would be there for Christmas. Tom never missed spending a Christmas with them, except when he was in Vietnam.

Jacob reached into the drawer beside the bed. He was tired from dancing and from his visit to Callie, but still he would read before sleeping. Callie's letter lay on top of the diary. Jacob opened it.

Dear Jake,

I have something to say to you, and it is, I believe, something you might wish to know. Please come back for a visit. It is about Drue. My dear Jacob, come soon.

Callie.

He had seen her and she had told him, and now what? It hadn't been for him what he had hoped. He wondered if he should call Molly, but decided to wait. The diary opened to spring 1944, and Jacob saw two entries on one page. They were dated a year apart.

May 1944

Jake leaves for France. I must not think about it too much. I will think instead about Molly and that baby. He is so small, not big like my babies were.

135

The next entry was only a few spaces down, but dated a year later:

June 1945

Jake got home today. He came to see his father. I was proud of him, the way he looked in his uniform. Karl talked to Jake for nearly two hours, but they didn't come out of that room. I don't know what they talked about. They probably just talked about the war. Jake goes to Virginia tomorrow. Molly and Joseph are waiting. Jake mentioned how he thought Karl looked better than he thought he would.

Karl didn't die for ten years. He stayed in that room. When he died, he was sixty. Jacob was already that age now. On the day Jacob returned for his father's funeral, Judge Bradford met him at the station.

Judge Bradford was not a bona fide judge, but a teacher whom everyone called Judge. As a boy, Jacob visited him in a one-room house and listened to stories the Judge told. He watched the palsy in the old man's hands. The room was full of sunlight in summer and whenever Jacob grew bored, he wandered to stand at the Judge's screen door and knock until he was heard.

"Come in," the Judge would say, "come in," and his hands went up, then fluttered down like two huge leaves. Usually, he offered Jake something to eat: meat from a can or cookies crumbly, stale. Some milk. Whenever Jacob's mother couldn't find him, she called the Judge.

"He's here, Sarah. Let him stay. I'll bring him home." And he told Jacob stories of Pandora, or the woman with a head of snakes, or the man who discovered fire. Jacob asked for these stories again and again.

There was a picture on the table beside the Judge's chair. It was of a young woman in a dance costume. Sometimes the Judge pointed to it so Jacob would notice and ask about her.

136

He had been married to her, but only for a short time. The Judge never talked about how she died. When Jacob looked at the picture, he didn't see how a woman like that could love the Judge. The Judge had a wen on his nose and one on his forehead, and his hands shook so badly. But Jacob's mother said that that wouldn't matter and that the Judge's wife loved him very much. The palsy wouldn't mean a thing.

On the day of his father's funeral, Jacob extended his hand to the Judge as he greeted him at the station. Jacob let the palsy of this man go through him, and felt in the firm hard palm a palpable goodness acquired from the Greek and Roman stories. The Judge had put those stories into the head of every child in town. But there was something else too, moving through his fingers, so that for the first time Jacob understood how the palsy wouldn't mean a thing.

When they arrived at the funeral home, the coroner had doctored Karl's appearance, but the face still sagged and the color beneath the dry pink chalk was gray. The room smelled of yeast and sweet powder.

The Judge waited outside, so Jacob looked a last time at his father's fixed face, fixing it in his own mind; but as he left, a day came to him as clear as any picture.

It was the day his father handed to him the label of a Robert Burns cigar, one that he had just opened. Jacob loved to watch his father open a cigar wrapper, because he did it with a slowness that made the act of smoking seem a small dance. And this day he opened it, pulling the light clear paper from around the cigar and slipping off the band. He always handed the band to Annie. She saved them. But this day Annie wasn't there, and Jacob felt sure that even if Annie had been standing right beside him that his father still would have handed it straight to him. Or if Drue had been there, his father would not have given it to Drue, or to anyone, only to Jacob. That was the way he handed it to him, with a sureness about who should have that insignia. Jacob had worn it all day until it tore in two, then he taped it and slipped it into his pocket. And though his father gave him other things over the years, nothing meant so much as did that small band.

February 11, 1956

We buried Karl. I knew it would come. I thought it would come before now. There is a relief, except that I know how lonely I will be. When it comes down to it, I think I might choose the hardship of looking after Karl (sick as he was), to being without him. Callie is still around. Annie is here. Jake came for the funeral, but he came alone since both the boys were sick. Molly sent a snapshot of Joseph, but none of Tom. Tom is seven. Joseph, almost twelve. Joseph still has that flu he's had all winter. Tom just has a cold.

Joseph would die that spring. So these things happened—deaths and births that came like a litany in Jacob's life.

Annie came in, still dressed for the celebration.

"You never said how Callie was." She was almost whispering.

"I said she was all right."

"Did she say what mother told her?"

Jacob had forgotten to ask. "No. She didn't."

"Well, I just wondered what it was." Annie's voice had the sound of someone who was more than just disappointed.

"We all have something to hide, I guess," Jacob ventured.

"I guess." Annie sat on the bed, weighting it slightly to one side. The light from the hallway hit her face like a spotlight. "I had another man once." She said it without hesitation and Jacob believed as she said it that Annie hoped it might be what her mother had done. "Which wouldn't be so bad, you know, except that Albert is like he is. That makes it worse."

"Who was it?" Jacob asked.

138

"John." She didn't say a last name, assuming either that Jacob knew who it was or that he shouldn't ask. "It was John. I loved him for the whole year I was thirty-eight years old. The first day I met him (he had been in town a week), he took me out to the tree that grows in that old silo." Jacob nodded, knowing where that was. "And when he reached for me, I pulled away." Annie didn't say how John's arms went into the air, high, and started to fall around her; but when Annie pulled away, he wrapped his arms around himself, hugging his chest. "He wouldn't look at me, but looked out the window and said he wanted us to know each other better. I leaned down over my knees and hugged them and decided to go with him. I had on a blue dress." Annie stroked the dress she wore now as if it were her blue one. When she looked again toward Jacob, her eyes were as round as a starving child's.

Jacob said, "What do you want me to say?"

"I think of Albert. What Albert would think."

"He knows, Annie."

"I don't believe that."

"Don't believe it then."

"Did he *tell* you?"

"When we went to Sophie's and Ned's one night—one night when you didn't go."

A smile came to Annie's lips. "Shouldn't have let you out of my sight."

"Naw." Jacob smiled back.

"How did he tell it?"

"Matter-of-factly. Said he was glad you did it that once, because he thought you wouldn't need to again."

"He was right." Annie stood up. "He was right about that." And the sureness of her statement made Jacob feel she had held up her thumb, as an artist would, to gauge with complete accuracy something Jacob had only looked at before.

* * *

139

It was after midnight when Jacob closed his mother's diary. He was more tired than he thought. As he turned out the light a sibilance moved quietly but persistently through his head, and he compared it to a faulty reed used in a flute, the sound produced being at once both promising and discordant.

He was glad Tom had decided not to come. As a boy Tom had liked to hunt, but since he spent time in Vietnam it seemed the idea of shooting or even holding a gun was a reminder too distasteful to think about.

"I got lost from my platoon," Tom told his parents upon returning from overseas, and he gave them a confession of sorts. "I wandered from town to town, but one night I found a small camp of people. Closest I ever came to getting shot. They were so quiet, I didn't even know they were there. There was an old couple, a young girl, and two boys about nine and thirteen."

They were in Vermont when Tom told this. He walked into the living room where his parents sat side by side on the sofa like two very young children who were about to be told a story. "The boys showed signs of malnutrition, the nine year old began to cough. They'd been hiding for days. I couldn't understand anyone's name, except the nine year old, who called himself Noley." Tom sat down and faced his parents. They could smell his favorite dinner cooking.

"They asked me to help them reach a boat which was two days' walk from where we were, so I went with them and carried Noley, rode him on my back. He coughed all the time and I could feel how hot he was through his clothes.

"It was late the next day when it happened. I think I saw before anyone else some men's shadows moving ahead of us in the woods. Without thinking, I ducked and when I did Noley fell off my back and woke, standing, dazed. I dragged him the fifty feet we had to go to get behind some bushes." Tom said now what he hated most to tell. "I was afraid Noley might go into one of his coughing fits before I laid him in a place in the bushes; so I covered his mouth with my hand and hoped he would sleep. He didn't cough, seemed to know he shouldn't, but I heard him swallow hard against the cough he felt rising.

"The others were talking to the men who stopped them in the road. I couldn't see from where I was. Noley burned with his fever and I was afraid he might grow delirious and begin to cry out. I was sure he would." At this, Tom's head dropped onto his chest and it seemed as though his head had been held up by a string that just now had come undone, making his head drop and nearly bounce. "I covered Noley's mouth with my hand, to protect us both. Then when I removed my hand, he was not moving at all. I didn't pay attention to that then." He sipped the drink his wife had brought to him.

"I went to see what happened to the others. I heard sounds, but couldn't really say what those sounds were. When I walked out, it must have been thirty minutes later. The bodies were in a huddle, gathered, as if for warmth, but their arms were thrown up in surprise.

"But the worst," he said, "the worst was what they did to the thirteen-year-old boy."

Jacob waved him off as if relieving Tom of the responsibility for telling this, but Tom continued, his voice picking up speed, going toward the end as quickly as he could. But even though his words came fast, his eyes held a glazed look.

"They had cut him." Tom barely whispered this.

Jacob leaned toward Tom so he could hear, but then grew still, not to hear, but thinking that moving might make things worse. He stiffened and finally asked. "And the others?"

"All dead."

"Noley?"

"When I went back to the branches where he was, I tried to wake him, but his mouth was open, his eyes were open, and his fever gone."

141

Jacob leaned back now, looking almost as if he were bored. And though the effect on him seemed to be something he had immediately forgotten, Molly told Tom that Jacob shared what happened to him as if it had been his own experience, or as if the children were his own. And there were nights as he lay dreaming, when Molly heard Jacob call out Noley's name.

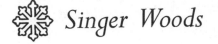 *Singer Woods*

On Sunday morning a snow began. Ned, Ned's boy Tim, Albert and twelve other men (some bringing their sons) left for deer camp. A little snow in November was so unusual that no one expected it to last. It didn't. It turned into sleet, then into rain and what had gathered on people's lawns and driveways in the early morning hours was gone by afternoon.

The men who arrived first at the camp built a fire and stacked food in the pantry so that when Minna, the cook, came in, she would have to do nothing but prepare the food. They could wake to fresh biscuits and at night have enormous cobblers filled with fruit and heavy crusts.

The ride to the camp was a four-hour drive. The cabin sat on a hundred-thousand-acre tract of land owned by a sewing machine company. Rent was paid each year by the hunters, but the group from Sweetwater had claimed the most desirable lot.

It was called Singer Woods and for many years men brought their sons to learn the fine points of hunting. Those boys would teach it too, when the time came. There were not many changes from year to year. These men did not like changes.

Jacob and Albert arrived with Soldier in the late afternoon. The men found bunks lined along the wall in the main room. Soldier chose a top bunk; Jacob took the bottom one. Each year the men brought Soldier. He carried a gun and walked with one of the better hunters. This year he would walk with Ned. The men took pride in teaching him and as Soldier showed progress, each man bragged about what he had taught.

The cabin was built on stilts, though a wide ramp was built for Albert's wheelchair. Albert's mistake had been simple. He grew impatient waiting to kill his first deer. He left the blind where he stood, and wandered to a section not assigned to him. He was hit low and at close range. A move behind a bush, a quick look for conspicuous clothing, then a shot. One man said he even called out and when he heard no answer, let go the shot that he hoped would bring the prize he wanted for his wall.

Albert's voice rang out through the woods, a cry like that of any wounded animal. When the men pushed aside the brush, they saw Albert sprawled, his eyes below them as wild as any deer's. And they called his name, *Albert*, over and over. It was their way of expressing apology and horror. Albert thought he might die, but when he woke, his legs were all that had gone. From the waist. He was twenty-three and had married Annie the year before. He wondered how he could live that way.

Annie was pregnant with their first child. And when she told Albert, she hoped it would give him reason to live. But it only drove him deeper into sorrow, making him question his ability to raise a family. He felt more inadequate than he was.

He did not go anywhere for a time. He worked and came home. When hunting season came around again, Annie sensed that he missed being part of it. The men in town built a blind that would hold his wheelchair. After another year, he went back. The men built ramps where they were needed and widened the path for him. That year Albert killed a fifteen point buck. It was a healing shot. After that, he went back every year.

A large pen held dogs by the name of Sally or Dot, and one named Singer—dogs bred for the purpose of hunting. They barked and jumped at the fence whenever anyone drove up.

Minna would not arrive until morning, so each man brought his first night's dinner which was prepared at home and brought cold in a sack. They planned strategies for the next morning's hunt and ate from their sacks. There was a briskness that hung around them, a liveliness that was credited to the weather, but had more to do with a sense of freedom and an absence of women. They went to bed and rose early, without bathing or changing their clothes.

Minna called them with a bell before it was light. A harsh call, but no complaints. Jacob, already up, had wandered outside. He liked the early darkness of these woods, and stopped about a hundred yards from the kitchen to grope for a tree. Nighttime here was different from any other nighttime he knew. It was almost salty. When Minna rang her bell, he was outside.

As he entered the kitchen door, Minna placed racks of biscuits into the oven. One rack was already done, and a redolence had reached the other room, making the men hurry. Minna offered Jacob a biscuit from the rack and he bounced it in his hands like a hot coal before he took a bite. Its texture was bready and by sophisticated standards not right, but it melted against his tongue as though it had been previously buttered. He nodded wide approval to Minna, who waited; but she turned her head as though his smile meant nothing.

In the other room men put on their long underwear, flannel shirts, layers of bright clothing, and heavy leather pants. They pushed shells into their pockets and dragged on their boots.

They ate Minna's breakfast and left it for her to clean up. It was the reason they brought her. Minna didn't mind, since she could clear and clean up their mess in record time. She would cook two large roasts and three hams. She would have a cobbler each night, varying the fruits. It was work she could do in her sleep and found it no trouble. She refused, though, to make their beds; but her refusal bothered no one. She spread her own bed neatly, fluffed the pillow and she wondered that they did not mind at night getting into unmade beds. She hoped they would not kill a deer.

They usually killed at least one deer, some years two or three. And they brought it to hang on a hook outside Minna's window, let it drain. The older men saw in the deer the performance of the hunt, a trophy; but the younger ones were not able to block out yet the sight of the animal they actually saw, not able to feel a pride in the kill, or to find pleasure in a power they did not yet need.

The boys would watch the men prepare the dead deer, first cutting off the head and hanging the deer by its feet to skin it. A rod was applied behind the ankle and Achilles tendon, so that the deer could be hung upside down. And while in that position, they cut open the deer's stomach to gut it, cleaning it out until it looked as empty and smooth as the inside of a balloon. Then they cut off its feet, front then back, so that as it hung upside down, its legs ended in blunt, ragged stubs. Sometimes, when the head was left on, the deer hung from its neck, so that the blood might drain without damaging the head for the taxidermist. And the same rod that was for the Achilles tendon would be stuck into the neck, and the deer's head would hang to the side like a sad child's. And the air kept it cold.

They hunted all morning, letting the dogs run the deer to them. They got some shots. Jacob heard the shooting, though he didn't fire any himself. At lunch, the conversation centered around what everyone had seen, how close they came, how big the deer was, trying to figure out if the deer Ned had seen was the same one Albert saw or if it was a different one.

Minna fixed cornbread, hash, and two huge bowls of custard for lunch. The men straggled in, ate, then left again, eating quickly in order to go back out. They were geared up and

146

bound to hunt till dark. Jacob lingered for about an hour before going back out, deciding finally to go another direction, to hunt squirrel or rabbit, something that would make him walk instead of wait. His legs became stiff when he sat for long periods of time, and they were stiff now. He took with him a few of the morning's biscuits, a pie slice of cornbread and a thermos of hot tea. He called good-bye to Minna.

Behind the cabin was a field, or a space that at one time had been a field. Now it was grown up with underbrush. Jacob wondered who lived in these woods, clearing this space for a place to live. It was one of the few spaces in these woods where the eyes could see for any distance at all and Jacob walked across it. He walked into the woods for an hour or so, he shot a few times at small game, killing a squirrel then tucking it into his back pouch. He could feel its warmth for a long time.

The smell of the woods grew stronger. Leaves soured with dampness and plants that could not grow in sunlight grew thick and close to the ground. Jacob kept walking, though there was no longer any path to help lead him out. He sat for a moment and when he did, remembered Callie's face. Not her face when he first saw her, but her face when she slept. For Jacob had gone back again to see Callie that night (though it was the middle of the night). He slept, woke after a few hours, and decided suddenly to go back. He wanted to ask Callie what his mother had told. Callie was asleep, so Jacob sat beside her, and that was the face that came back to him now—Callie sleeping.

He began to walk again. He knew he had gone too far. He started to turn back, but the light became more slanted. It was late. Jacob didn't want to admit he was confused as to whether he was leaving the woods or going deeper into them. And though it was still early, it was nearly dark, for the forest found its darkness before the fields.

The terrain of the forest had changed, become more hilly,

147

rocky; and Jacob found himself climbing small ridges (not to see anything, for the forest was too dense, but to get over the ridge). He could not see the forest's edge, nor any sign of a road, and the sounds and smells were stronger here than any he had ever encountered. He climbed and walked and called, but heard only his own voice returning from a hill, or ridge. He felt glad he had brought the cold biscuits and thermos, and was sorry he had already eaten the pie-shaped cornbread. He would ration the rest. A small cavelike opening seemed a good place to stop. He should sleep. Certainly he was tired enough. The sky was full of stars and there was no trace now of sunlight.

He pulled from his pocket one biscuit and opened it as he would open a book, then put half of it back and ate, chewing slowly to savor the dry taste. He wished he had worn a warmer coat, and wished even more for a cover for his legs. He did not have his warm hip boots, because they were too bulky to bring on the train. His legs began to stiffen in the cold night air, so he covered them with his arms, hugging himself to get warm. It was not a comfortable position, but he dozed awhile and felt sure someone would find him soon.

He woke as though someone had called to him. He said, "What?" and when he woke his shoulders ached as deeply as they had ever ached, piercing even to his elbow and forearm, as if he carried a great weight. And as he straightened his back with effort, he both felt and heard a harsh grinding sound like the turning of an ice-cream freezer done by hand. Then it changed in seconds to something shrill, almost witchlike, and he turned to see a wild cat as large as a dog fix his claws into his arm, going at first for the squirrel he could smell at Jacob's back, but then going for Jacob himself. Jacob jerked but the cat went for his throat. He pulled away soon enough to save himself from a quick death, the cat knowing more about killing than Jacob did. The cat clung to his arm. Jacob shook him loose until the cat had hold of only his hand, but held with all

148

the power his jaws had. So with his other hand, Jacob reached for a knife he used to clean and cut open small game, and he buried the knife into the cat's back, ripping it downward with a tear that came out in the wild cat's last cry. And the cat's head beside Jacob lay so steeped in surprise at what had been dealt that Jacob leaned his own head to see, explain. And though dark was predominant and the starlight could not show much, Jacob saw the cat pull back his claws to cover his chest, a gesture made after death, protecting himself from more harm, as though more harm could make him worse because he was gone, already gone before the cry was fully finished. Jacob saw him fall backward and it was at that moment that his arm began to throb where the cat had held on. His coat protected him some, but not enough to prevent the cat from making a gash that tore Jacob's upper arm, the way one might cut a loaf of bread down the middle instead of slicing it. But his hand felt numb, his fingers chewed as if by a machine, and he was surprised how, right then, there was almost no pain from those mangled fingers. But it came later.

He removed his coat and tore his shirt to make a bandage from a piece of his sleeve. He wished it were morning and the sun could warm him, but the night still had more hours, and Jacob began to talk to himself, give himself hope. He talked to parts of his body, cursing his legs for being old and his shoulders for aching.

He could feel the blood hardening onto his knuckles and crusting at his elbow. He leaned back onto the rock. The cat lay beside him, but Jacob didn't want to look, his squirrel still tucked inside the back pouch. Jacob reached for another biscuit, not opening it or rationing it, but placing it whole into his mouth. His arm trembled as he lifted the thermos to his lips.

He hoped someone would come soon. He slept, but heard, as the day came up, a noise on the rise not two hundred feet from him. He flinched and moved back, before he saw coming

149

up from the bushes, antlers bigger than most deer. At first he thought it was an elk, but this was not country for elk; and now the animal was high enough that Jacob could see the throat, and there was no waddle there beneath the neck. It was a mule deer, bigger than he had ever seen, and he hoped to kill it.

Jacob's first deer had come up over a rise such as this one had done, but Jacob did not kill it. He wanted to prove himself at sixteen, to bring home a prize, but he didn't take his chance and instead watched the thing he wanted most walk away. What he thought would be glory turned to shame.

The men called it Buck Fever and most had had the experience. But today, with one arm no good to him and his legs stiff from cold, he scooted his gun, anchored it to his shoulder and shot, left-handed, though he never had. And he had never shot at this close range before, so he hoped it would not be unsportsmanlike, hoped it would not tear the deer apart in an ungainly way.

When the deer turned its head, Jacob did not move, except his finger that pulled and blew the shot from Jacob's gun as straight toward that mule deer's heart as it would go. And the deer fell, or rather crumpled without a sound.

Then Jacob stood with effort, telling his legs to go that two hundred feet to see what he had shot, his pain dissolving in the excitement. The mule deer's eyes were open, his head especially large. And Jacob knew he could never lift those legs and pull them to his shoulders, draping the animal around his neck as he used to do. He remembered the collar of flesh around him, too heavy now to be supported by these legs.

Another sound made him turn, not as quickly as he meant to, but quick enough to see hunters who had heard his shot.

"You get one?" one man asked.

"Yeah." Jacob turned all the way around. They could see his coat, his bandage.

"My God, man. You been out here all night?"

But Jacob wasn't answering. He looked down to inspect his hand as though he had forgotten about it.

"What happened?" another man asked.

"Where's your camp? You at Ned Wise's camp?" Jacob shook his head yes.

"The group from Sweetwater," he heard someone say. But it was the last thing he heard.

They took Jacob to his camp and Ned drove him to the hospital. The others brought the mule deer back for him in a truck. They skinned it and hung it outside Minna's window.

 *A Second Sleep*

Jacob woke under the anesthetic. He didn't remember being taken to the hospital, nor did he remember being lost, or hunting, killing a deer. He lay with his arms strapped on a hard table and for a long time he could hear voices in a conversational tone. He could not tell how long he dozed. It seemed only a few moments, but one time when he woke, his hand was bandaged and bottles with tubes were connected to his arm. He tried to get up and heard himself say he wanted to get out of there.

Several people rushed to him saying, "Mr. Bechner," in measured voices. When he dismantled the bottle above him, two doctors came. They strapped him down again. One told him he was fine and that he should sleep now. The other said not to knock over the bottles again because they had a tough time finding a vein that time and the bottle needed to be up for another forty-eight hours. Jacob lay back and decided to take the nourishment.

Once he thought he heard Molly, but it was a nurse he had never seen before. Another time he felt Callie's strong hands against his neck, kneading his back.

"Is your Mama home?" Callie would ask.
"I think so."
Sarah was always home. Sarah was a woman who had not

grown bitter with age. When she spoke, her body held an inclination to it, a bend toward whomever was speaking, and she gave the impression of intense interest. She was a stout woman, her face round, her cheeks soft pads that she pressed against her children's foreheads when they were sick. Her eyes were dull blue circles that could look into Jacob or anyone, seeming at those times enormous and sure.

"Bechner?"

"Yes."

"You are the family of Karl Bechner?"

"Jacob."

"Huh?"

"I'm Jacob. Karl Bechner was my father."

"Ah." His head went back as if he had seen something above Jacob's head. "Well, maybe I should talk with the lady of the house."

"My mother," Jacob told him, "is in the kitchen." He motioned for the man to come in. "I'll get her."

"Mrs. Bechner?" the man asked, watching Sarah approach him. She wiped her hands on her apron. Sarah didn't answer audibly, but shook her head once to acknowledge him and kept wiping her hands. "Maybe we could sit down," he said. He carried a briefcase. "My name is Holden. Alfred Holden. I'm with the American Life and Mutual Insurance Company. Out of Memphis."

"Memphis?" Sarah sat before he did. It was as though she had never heard of Memphis.

"And I've brought your settlement." Then he said, "I'm sorry," in a professionally apologetic tone of voice, "that it took so long, but we had a lot of things to consider, you know—whether or not Mr. Bechner, your husband," he looked down to the paper he had removed from his briefcase, "had kept up his policy, made each payment on time, all of that."

"Yes." Sarah looked as if she might still be wondering about

153

Memphis. Then Alfred E. Holden (his name embossed in gold lettering on his briefcase) handed Sarah a check. Jacob looked over her shoulder to read the amount, but it did not actually register at first. They only saw a four and a five, and three zeros.

"Mr. Bechner was faithful to this policy. Took it out in 1931 and paid on it regular all those years."

"When was Karl ever in Memphis?" Sarah asked no one in particular.

"We went to Memphis once when he was sick," Jacob remembered.

"When was that?"

When was he *not* sick? Jacob had not said it, but thought it. His mother read his face.

"Not that." She remembered. "He had pneumonia once. They took him to the hospital, then took him to Knoxville. But he had to go all the way to Memphis before he got well." She decided Karl had taken out the policy on himself after he got well in Memphis. And during those years he stayed in his room (drinking, not doing anything), he had done that one thing, for them all, had left this gift.

"Thank you, Mr. Holden." Sarah stood up and handed the check to Jacob, as if it were a drawing shown to her by a child she didn't know very well and felt she had given enough attention to it. She showed Mr. Holden to the door and walked back to the kitchen.

In his anesthetized sleep Jacob dreamed of his mother and of Callie passing him on the road or in his home. Of Drue going down the river, his sleep being like that ride.

"What would you have done though, if I hadn't?"

"If you hadn't come up?"

"Yeah."

"I would've gone in after you. Jumped in, pulled you up."

And he thought of the young girl who reached into the

alligator's mouth, what happened to her. In his sleep, Jacob wondered again how that girl could be all right.

But Jacob was all right. He woke completely and was all right. He could not imagine what time of the day it was, until Cedar and Ty came and told him they had just eaten supper. They stared at Jacob's hand as though someone told them not to mention it unless he did.

"It's not so bad," he told them. "I lost three fingers, but not all the way." Still the children didn't know what to say. "It's not so bad," he said again and pretended to poke at them as though he wore a boxing glove. They dodged and began to tell about themselves, what they had been doing, and they told him as though he had been waiting to hear. But after a while, they asked him questions.

"Does it hurt?" Ty asked.

"Yes. Some." Jacob rubbed his arm above the bandage. "But it won't hurt like this for long."

"How long?" Cedar wanted to know.

"I don't know." Jacob began to describe to the children the phenomenon of phantom pain, how even though the fingers were no longer there, the pain stayed. He said how he could feel those fingers there, and at times they might hurt or ache or itch. The children were fascinated as though he told them a magic trick. Jacob thought for a moment that this may have been the bragging the little girl had done, her arm part gone and people like Drue telling how she bragged. He wondered now with Cedar and Ty if he might be playing it for all it was worth. He thought maybe he was.

But Cedar and Ty loved to hear about phantom pain, and Jacob found that the telling of it relieved him some, so he told it each time. As the pain left him, he missed it, imagining that if the pain was felt maybe there was a chance again for wholeness, but when it had gone, he would be left with only those stubs that he would learn to use with deftness and coordination.

* * *

155

It was later when Jacob went into a second sleep. He dreamed (this dream not so much a remembering dream, but a journey) about something he had never done, or even thought about having to do.

He dreamed that he and his mother went to identify Drue's body. That after the fire, he had been asked to see the body and tell whether or not it was his brother, was Sarah's son. He had never done that, though his mother had, and his father. His mother had described it. His father never mentioned it.

This morgue, where Jacob had never been, was a long narrow building with steps leading to it. Jacob saw it only from the outside, but here in his second sleep, he entered it. And he smelled the odor of formaldehyde and treated skin. He walked with his mother down the corridor. He walked slightly in front of her. The room to his right had a door partially open and Jacob leaned to see in. He leaned without having to take any steps toward the door as sometimes happens in dreams. And he could see the entire room, though his mother was behind him now and could see nothing. Jacob could hear her telling him to come on, as she went toward another room at the end of the hall. They passed rooms where people worked. Sometimes the doors were open, sometimes closed. Jacob could see men and women looking under microscopes, cleaning tables, carrying sheets to be used or that had already been used. One man carried a large bucket down the hallway and out the door that led to the back. His mother didn't turn either way, but looked straight ahead. And even in this dream, Jacob wondered what his father had done.

They entered a room with tables scattered and one table with a stack of sheets. Other tables were not thoroughly cleaned. Drue lay on a slab of what seemed to be rock, but which was much like every table.

"Here," the man said, who had been guiding them through the corridors.

There Drue lay. He was covered completely, but the man brought the sheet down to Drue's waist and Jacob saw, without recognizing, the flesh raw and black, peeled down at places like old rind. Jacob searched for a wound, his eyes searched again and again, but found nothing, only his brother's flesh blackened, and the fetid odor that was covered (though not completely) with chemical.

His mother stood beside him, very still. Jacob kept thinking she would scream or something, cry, do something. She stood and with concentration searched Drue's body for marks that might tell her this was, was not, her son. What she said, she had really said, but had said it at the funeral home, when they went to see the body. By then, it was already prepared.

"I knew by the way he was lying there," she said. "The way his head and feet were, I knew. I would've known him anywhere." And she kept repeating the recognition of her son, feeling some connection in knowing him even in this condition. Most of his skin was gone. And she said how she wished the fireman hadn't hosed him down that way, because she thought the firemen had done it, but it was Doc who had washed off so much of the skin. And she spoke matter-of-factly, as if she felt something had been ruined by hosing him down.

"Well, they had to," Jacob had told her, and told her again in his dream.

The dream made a quick shift to Drue's grave and though there were many people there that day, there was no one with him in his dream. Everything seemed unusually large, the trees, the casket Drue lay in, the tent above the grave that protected them from rain or ruin. And even Jacob felt large in a strange way, looming almost as the trees did. He moved to watch the casket lowered, not seeing anyone there to lower it, not lowering it himself, though watching it move downward. And though it was closed, sealed, it seemed that Jacob could see to the satin-lined place where Drue lay in his Sunday

157

clothes, his ruined face. The birthmark now completely gone, burned clean. And Jacob could see, as he moved closer, his own inexplicable portrait.

When he awoke, he was surrounded by nurses and doctors, who were angry at him for knocking down every bottle and for tearing the straps on his arms and waist. He had broken his wrist straps completely loose from the table.

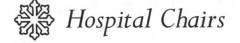 *Hospital Chairs*

"Let's take these chairs and go out into the hallway."
Molly pointed to a short hall that seemed not to be busy. Annie
picked up a chair to follow her. They propped the chairs
against the wall and situated themselves.

"Now," said Molly. Molly arrived in Sweetwater hours after
she heard the news about Jacob. She knew only that he had
hunted and that serious damage was done to his hand. She
knew he might lose the use of it. "Now," she said again, sitting,
turning to Annie, as if this was what she had been waiting for,
to sit here in this hallway. And, in fact, during her ride here,
she *had* thought of talking to Annie. But she didn't start right
away with what she wanted to say, instead she mentioned
Callie.

"Jake got a letter from Callie."

Annie nodded. "People say she's crazy."

"May be. But she wrote the letter. She sent the clipping
about Drue."

Annie uncrossed her legs, then crossed them again and
leaned hard against the straight-backed chair, not comfortable
and not likely to be in that hallway. They both turned to see
Albert in the waiting room.

"So," Molly continued, "did Jake see Callie before he went
hunting?"

"The night of the dance," Annie said. "I urged him to go

159

to her house, and thought she might come back with him. She usually comes to those things, but didn't that night."

Molly waited for more, then asked, "And when he came back?" Her question implied maybe that Jacob's injury had something to do with what Callie had told him, not the way she asked, but her riddled expression.

"He came back without her, but he'd seen her." Then Annie added, "He seemed all right then."

Molly shifted in her chair. Annie shifted too, and the shifting allowed them to move on to what they wanted to say. Both of them poised, each wanting to tell something to the other. Annie spoke first.

"There's something you never knew, I think."

Molly thought Annie might tell what Jake had already told her in the station house. "Yes, I know," she said.

"There was a child there that night. He saw everything. Saw it all." There was no need to identify the night Annie was talking about.

"A child?" Molly leaned forward in her chair, trying to whisper, but she didn't whisper. "A child?"

"The child opened the gun case before Drue got home and then ended up shooting Drue. When he ran out, he pulled down the curtain and it caught fire. But he hadn't meant to do any of it. It just happened like that."

"What child?"

"Oh, he isn't a child anymore. A grown man. The Judge decided he shouldn't be jailed, or even blamed. It was innocent, though what it caused wasn't." Annie looked to the floor.

Molly wondered if Annie wished for punishment of that child. "What about you? What did you think?"

"No, no." Annie looked up, but not at Molly. "That's not it." They both watched a nurse carry a tray of pills with cups of water into a room near them. "I didn't think he should be punished. Judge Bradford told me never to mention it. I've never told. Callie knew about it. The Judge is dead and Callie will soon be gone herself, so I consider the secret now to be almost forgotten." Annie seemed to be forgetting that she had just told Molly, that now Molly was included in this comradeship, like patriots together in a foreign country. "And the child," Annie added, forgetting too that the child was no longer a child. Annie leaned forward onto her knees. "Doc knew, of course. He took care of Drue after the fire."

"Who told you? Were you there?"

"No. I never knew until years later. Mary Hatley told me. One Sunday afternoon she told me and I asked the Judge and he said that was right." It occurred to Molly that everyone might know of Jacob's innocence, except Jacob himself.

"It's a funny thing to think about sometimes," Annie continued, as though she were telling part of the same thing, "you know, Jake used to play the piano." Molly didn't know this, nor did she know why Annie was saying it now. "Though Drue was the one who loved music."

Molly *did* know that Drue loved music. He had come to her house in the days before she was married and told her he wanted to study music and that he might leave Sweetwater. Sometimes he brought a record to let her hear it.

"Our father never wanted me to play the piano," Annie said. "Or Drue either. Only Jake. But Jake never did like it." She sat back now, then said (as though this were not the important part at all), "Our father would say 'Listen, listen to this Jake,' and he'd play something so Jake would listen, but Jake wouldn't understand what he was supposed to hear. And my father would raise his eyebrows at a certain part to make sure Jake knew what he meant, so Jake nodded as though he did. But you could tell, you could tell he didn't. And Jake always pretended to understand more about music than he really did. Drue was the one who understood." Molly saw that the reason for saying this was because Annie still missed Drue. Then

161

Annie turned and faced Molly as though it might be her turn to tell something.

"Drue came to my house the night he died," said Molly, and she saw that Annie didn't know, or even expect this, because her look was fatuous, as if Molly had begun to speak a foreign language. "He was there before the fire," she said. "They argued. Jake and Drue. At my house." Her mouth distorted as she said the words, the way a mouth distorts when pulled with sadness. "*Before.*" Then she told the whole thing.

"Drue came by sometimes, but usually he came in the daytime. It was almost seven o'clock that night, and my family had gone out. So I was there alone. Drue came to tell me he wanted to leave Sweetwater, to go somewhere, he didn't know where. He wanted to study music." Molly's face grew pale, her emotions augmented by what she would tell and wondering whether or not she should tell it. But something had started here in these chairs, and whatever was being said would not be stopped now. Not now.

"I asked if he wanted me to warm up some soup I had. We went to the kitchen. Drue took a fat slice of bread I'd baked, but was stale. He said it was good." She smiled remembering this, so Annie smiled too. "We talked awhile about where Drue might go, then he asked if I was sure I wanted to get married. Because Jake and I were getting married in the summer and this was the spring. But he didn't mention Jake, just asked, as if I might be marrying somebody he didn't know. I said I was sure, but when I said it he drew me to him. I was standing at the table and he sat with his elbows on the oilcloth. I had just sliced another hunk of bread and put it on a small plate in front of him. I could hear the soup boiling behind me. And Drue, he pushed the plate with the bread on it away from him. At first, I thought it was rude to do that, but he did it so slowly that I wondered if he wasn't feeling well, was sick. So I said, 'Drue? Are you sick?' and I've thought so many times that it was the last thing I said to him directly. I stood for a moment thinking he would tell me. But when he turned, he didn't look at my face, he looked at my waistline where I had an apron tied double around myself. He untied it and took it off, his arms reaching around me once to loosen. Then he buried his head in that part of my dress. I didn't know what to do, so I held his head with both my hands. We were like that when Jake came in. The apron on the floor. And there were a few moments when I think our spirit left our bodies, went somewhere to be for a while, because our bodies brimmed with the pain of seeing each other in ways we didn't expect, and in misunderstanding and confused caring for one another.

"Drue stood up and said 'I'm sorry' which implied a kind of guilt, though nothing happened but his movement toward me. Jake asked what we were doing, he asked quietly at first, then he repeated the question with an almost primal quality that made me fall back, fall back against the refrigerator. I think that maybe he even pushed me.

"Then Jake hit Drue. Drue didn't fight back. Jake hit him again, and the only sound was the sound of Jake's fist against Drue's bone and ear. Drue hummed and whimpered like a child caught stealing. That's how they left each other. Drue leaving the house quickly, and me trying to talk to Jake. His eyes have never been so blind, so wild. I was able, after a while, to explain that though Drue had pulled me to him, had held me for a moment, that it was nothing. I told him how it was one of those isolated moments people feel, but don't usually act upon, and how it didn't matter. But it was not until after I had said all that that Jake calmed down. He went that night to Drue's house to apologize." Molly dropped her head. "I didn't know, ever know, Drue was shot. Now I've known it twice in only a few weeks, wondering in these weeks if Jake had in fact done it, suffering in a short time the way Jake suffered all these years. And now," she looked to Annie, "this boy. Who is he?

163

He must still live here." Annie nodded and started to tell, but Molly hadn't finished and said one more thing about Jake.

Annie didn't hear. "No," she said. "The young boy. He bore it all." And even now she didn't want to tell, the name coming out on her tongue slowly and without ease. "Oliver Brise," she told. "It was Soldier."

It was four-thirty when the doctors came out and told them that Jacob would be all right, that they had taken off three of his fingers, but only to the second knuckle and that it would not handicap him too much. The doctor put his own hand into the position that Jacob's hand would look like normally. And both women pushed forward in their hospital chairs to try and imagine it.

❊ *Like Men Anywhere*

It was two days later when Soldier came to see Jacob, walked the fifteen blocks it took to get to the hospital. When he entered Jacob's room, the nurse had set lunch on the table beside the bed. Soldier stood in the doorway.

"Come in," said Jacob. The nurse left. Soldier looked ragged, his clothes in disorder.

"Did you deliver your papers?"

Soldier shook his head. "I will though." He was out of breath and Jacob knew he had walked all the way without stopping, or thinking to give himself a rest and that probably he had gotten lost a couple of times and that had made it even longer, because Soldier looked so glad to finally be here. Jacob told him to sit down and Soldier sat on the bed. He pointed to Jacob's bandaged hand and wanted to ask something.

"The hunting trip," Jacob told him. "A wildcat came from behind. I was lucky."

Soldier frowned at the bandage and asked why that was lucky.

"Well, he could've killed me. He went for my throat. I had to fight him off."

"Oh."

"What's the matter?" Jacob asked him. Soldier didn't come, Jacob thought, to ask about my hand. His jacket was torn and his pants dirty. Jacob wondered where he had been.

165

"What happened?" And he thought of the two men at the celebration and began to search Soldier's face for marks of a fight, or other signs.

Soldier was about to speak, so Jacob asked again what happened and then asked if it had to do with the men at the celebration. When he asked this, Soldier's body bent over as though he had been hit from the front, and was protecting himself. Jacob laid one hand on Soldier's back. He patted him as if Soldier were a small child.

"They took me out," Soldier finally said from between his knees. And the surface of his voice offered a sound that set Jacob swimming, a deep chord, accurate in emotion. Soldier had mud caked on his shoes, and some on his back.

"They push you down?" Jacob asked, brushing Soldier off, hoping that was all they did, suspecting it wasn't. "They hurt you?" Soldier shook his head but kept it down. He pointed to the sleeve of his coat. It was torn.

"We can fix it," Jacob said.

"They said they'd show me some sheep," Soldier began. "I said I'd seen some. They said I'd never seen one this big." Soldier started to cough, choke, but it was more than that. He sobbed in a way that wrenched him. "They seemed nice. I thought they would really like me now. I thought that other night I showed them what a man I was and that they liked me for that. They even said it, said I was a man now and I had proved it. Now I would prove it again. With them." Soldier sat upright. "And we could be friends, like men anywhere."

Jacob knew that these men had found Soldier in his apartment or on the apartment steps. And they had insisted in a genial way that Soldier could be their friend now. That was what Soldier wanted—to be friends with other men, man to man, like men anywhere. And what he hated most was to be treated as Jacob treated him, as a small child. Jacob removed his hand from Soldier's back. "I'm sorry," he said.

"That's okay." Soldier forgave him, without knowing exactly what he forgave, and Jacob wanted to make it clear, but instead asked, "What did they do?"

"We went toward Murfreesboro, not that far, but that direction because I saw some signs." Jacob didn't realize Soldier could read road signs. "Then we turned to a farm road, dirt. No farmhouse, just road. It led to a field where there were some cows, but I didn't see any sheep. The cows were white and the men pointed and said 'There,' and they pointed at the cows. I said 'That's not sheep, that's cows.' And they laughed loud, said how I didn't know anything, that that was sheep, and didn't I know the difference. I said I did and that I wanted to go home. But they kept laughing. Then they started acting nice again and said they would teach me something. I got out of the car and one jerked my jacket." Soldier reached up to his shoulder and showed Jacob again the torn place. Jacob fingered it as though he hadn't noticed it before.

"And they pushed me to that field and they laughed and I knew they would do something but I didn't know what. They said 'You ever had a woman, Soldier?' And I knew what they meant, but I never had. And they said, 'This is just like having a woman. You can come out here anytime, and it won't hurt nobody. We're doing you a favor, boy. We're gonna show you how.' So I started yelling and telling them to leave me alone. And I didn't even want them to take me home, I just wanted to leave. 'Let me walk back,' I said. But they laughed louder and louder. 'You gonna have trouble walking after this,' one said. And they pulled down my pants." He leaned forward again. His face shuddered at the hairline.

"I know. I know." Jacob didn't want to hear more, but would listen if Soldier told.

"And they kept calling those cows sheep." Soldier spoke now to the clean linoleum floor. "They called me over, and they pulled down their pants and showed me how."

"They make you do it?" Jacob asked.

Soldier shook his head. "I got away," he said. "I ran off."

167

Jacob sat there, propped against two pillows, trying to think of what to tell Soldier. "It doesn't matter," he said, but it was only half of what he wanted to say, not knowing all of it yet.

"And they asked me what I was carrying," Soldier said, telling something that happened earlier. "I told them 'Nothing.' And it was the second time they asked that and the second time I answered." Soldier waited a moment to see if Jacob could explain, but Jacob couldn't; nor could he figure where in the conversation it fit.

So Jacob said again, "It doesn't matter," thinking as he said it that surely it *did* matter, and that Soldier's open, wounded face told him it did matter. Then he said, "Forget about it, Soldier. You are a fine man, a good man."

Soldier stood up now, stronger. "Yes," he said, believing maybe he *was* a man.

"Did you walk back?" Jacob asked, finding he didn't want to speak of this anymore and wished Soldier would leave. Soldier looked so tired.

"Another car came by," said Soldier. "They stopped and said 'Want to get in, Soldier?' But I didn't know who it was, so I didn't. They went on. I was glad." Soldier walked to the window to look out. "But when I got home, those men had been there. Messed up my room." He wanted to tell Jacob something else, but didn't. "They broke my lock."

"We can fix it," said Jacob.

And Jacob thought of Soldier, left in the grass of that field, then walking back along the road at night, cold and damp. He asked Soldier if he had been afraid walking back and if he had been cold. Soldier said he had not been afraid, but he had been cold, though the cold felt good to him then, and the night was clear and he liked looking at the stars, and the moon was full and he liked looking at that too, because it made him forget. And Jacob knew how a moon on a cold clear night could excuse anything.

168

 *Going After Humbaba*

Because Molly knew that Jacob would need to recuperate and be seen again by the doctors, she left him at
Annie's house. It was almost Thanksgiving, and she told Annie
some of the special dishes Jacob liked. Annie promised to make
them for him. "He'll be fine," Annie said. "You call him on
Thanksgiving."

"I need to get back," Molly said. It was an apology. "I told
the school I'd be back at the end of this week." Molly taught
in the same school where Jacob taught, and had even taken
over some of his classes this semester. That way they would
not lose the money he would have lost by taking the semester off.

"Now he'll be fine," Annie told her. "You go. And call him
on Thanksgiving."

Now it was Thanksgiving, and Cedar and Ty were having
dinner with them. So was Soldier. Molly had already called
once to say she would be eating with a neighbor and she would
call again later to ask what Annie had prepared. Jacob would
tell her Annie made for him everything Molly suggested, but
that it wasn't as good as when Molly made it.

After their big meal, Jacob called the children to his room.
Soldier followed. Jacob wanted to tell them a story. Not a
porch story, but one taught in his classroom. Soldier and Ty
settled in chairs to listen. Cedar sat on the edge of Jacob's bed.

Jacob began. "Gilgamesh was a great builder."

"Did you make up that name?" Cedar doubted him.

"No, that's part of the story. Gilgamesh was strong and powerful, more than anyone else." Soldier nodded to indicate he liked that beginning, wishing, Jacob guessed, that he himself were Gilgamesh, or at least strong and powerful. But, of course, they would all wish it before the story was through.

"He was the king of Uruk."

"I'm cold," said Ty. He pulled the electric heater close to him. Annie's house was so old that heat and cold invaded each room and she had heaters scattered about the house in winter, fans in summer. The heater in Jacob's room was the largest and glowed like a huge red coal. Jacob warned Ty not to sit too close.

"The king was wise and knew secret things."

"Like what?" Cedar asked.

Jacob was sorry he had begun the story, forgetting the interruptions of the young. "Well, like he would know somebody was coming to see him even before they came."

"How'd he know that?"

"He just did. For one thing, he was two-thirds god and one-third man."

Soldier laughed, picturing who knows what.

"And he built walls," Jacob continued, hoping at some point to catch their attention. "He was a builder."

"You already said that." Ty got up again to move the heater a little closer to him and to the bed.

"Anyway," said Jacob, "the people of Uruk said that Gilgamesh was *too* strong, said he needed an equal, and they asked the goddess of creation to create someone equal to Gilgamesh." Jacob waited to see what new interruption might occur. Nothing. "So. The goddess took the stuff from the earth and dipped it in water and pinched off the clay and let it fall in the wilderness. That's how Enkidu was created."

"Did you make that name up?"

170

"What? Enkidu?"

Cedar nodded.

"No. That was his name." He wished she would listen without interrupting. "Now, Enkidu's body was rough. He had hair as long as a woman's, in fact, his whole body was covered with hair. He ate grass in the hills and went to the water hole with other animals."

"Are these *real* people?" Ty asked.

"Well, he was more like an animal," Jacob said, ignoring the question. "But one day a trapper from town saw Enkidu at the water hole and returned home to say that there was a man who lived and ate like the animals, and that he must be the strongest man in the world. He told how this wild man protected other animals from traps that were set out, so that the trapper could not catch anything.

"The trapper's father said 'Go to Gilgamesh and tell him, then get a harlot and bring her back to this wild man. Let her tame him.' " Jacob shifted in the bed, wondering why he had used that word. "So they brought this woman and left her there in the wilderness and she lived with the wild man for a while, until all the other animals saw that Enkidu was not an animal at all. And they rejected him."

"Where did Harlot go?" Cedar asked, as if she had said somebody's name.

Jacob put his hand on her knee. "Try not to interrupt, honey."

"Harlot," Jacob said, deciding to leave it at that, "stayed with Enkidu for six days and seven nights and when Enkidu went back to the beasts they ran from him. It was then that Enkidu realized he could no longer run fast. He had become weak, because now he had wisdom and the thoughts of a man, and a man's heart. Harlot told Enkidu to come to Uruk with her and meet Gilgamesh. So Enkidu went, because he wanted more than anything for someone to understand his heart.

"Harlot told Enkidu how strong and wise Gilgamesh was.

171

She said 'Even now he'll know you are coming.' And sure enough, Gilgamesh had a dream. He dreamt of a meteor made from the stuff of the earth, and when it fell, he tried to lift it, but it was too heavy. He felt love for it and brought it to his mother. She said the reason he loved it was because it was like a brother to him. His mother told him that the piece that fell in his dream was a strong comrade. Then Gilgamesh had a second dream and in it was an ax. He loved that too, loved it like a woman, or like himself. Again, his mother told him that it was the companion-brother, who was to be Enkidu."

"*I* dream sometimes." Ty.

"*I* do too." Soldier.

"Harlot brought Enkidu to town and taught him how to eat bread and drink wine. Enkidu put on clothes, but still he didn't meet Gilgamesh, until one day he heard a complaint about Gilgamesh as a king, so Enkidu decided to make himself the king. Gilgamesh and Enkidu met. They fought, or rather they had a wrestling bout. Gilgamesh won. After that, they became friends."

Cedar moved from the foot of Jacob's bed to the middle. "I'm *hot*. Ty, move that heater away from me before my legs burn off." Ty scooted the heater away with his foot, but only about an inch. "Ty!" He moved it another inch.

Soldier said, "Gilgamesh and Enkidu became friends." He wanted to get back to the story, but hadn't pronounced the names right. He started to rock back and forth.

"One day Gilgamesh told Enkidu, 'Let's go to the Country of the Living or, as it was also called, The Land of the Cedars.'" Cedar smiled and turned to the others as though she should be given special recognition.

"Gilgamesh wanted to use the cedars to build a monument to the gods. But," and Jacob paused for emphasis, "there lived in that forest where the cedars were a ferocious giant named Humbaba. He was evil."

Cedar believed it all now.

"Enkidu told how big the forest was and that he had been there and had lived with the wild beasts. He told how Humbaba guarded the cedars and described Humbaba saying, 'He roars like a storm, his breath is like fire, and his jaws are death itself.' "

Soldier said Yes, showing he understood.

"You see," Jacob continued, "Humbaba means Hugeness and he guarded the cedars so well that if anything stirred in the forest, no matter where or how far off, Humbaba heard. Enkidu was worried and he told Gilgamesh to ask the Sun God for help, because the country of the cedars belonged to the Sun God. The Sun God promised the strongest of help. He gave Gilgamesh all the winds."

"He gave the wind." Soldier tried to picture that as a gift. His forehead implored Jacob to make it clearer.

"He gave the north wind, whirlwind, icy wind, scorching wind, all of them. Then he ordered weapons to be made, and Gilgamesh announced that he was going to fight Humbaba. The people were afraid and warned him not to go. But Gilgamesh said," Jacob clearly loved this part, "Gilgamesh said, you know what he said?"

Cedar said she didn't know, and Ty had stood up to move his chair again, but was sitting down. Soldier rocked forward.

"He said, 'What should I do? Say I'm *afraid* of Humbaba? Should I sit home all the rest of my life?' "

Soldier shook his head, as if the question were meant for him.

"Now they were ready to get their weapons—swords, arrows, bows. Gilgamesh took an ax. When they left, the people warned him not to trust too much in his own strength, to let Enkidu lead the way. Because Enkidu already knew the forest and had seen Humbaba and was experienced in battles. So you see," Jacob pushed with his hands to sit up straighter in

173

the bed, forgetting about his injury. But when he pushed, he winced with pain that that gesture caused him, so that everyone forgot the story and hoped Jacob's hand was all right. "Gilgamesh," he continued, "knew the dream, but Enkidu knew the work."

"You better watch out about your hand," said Cedar, still looking at Jacob's brow. Jacob had thought it would be fun to tell them this story, but that had been knocked completely over.

"I wish ya'll would *listen*," Jacob told them, his first outburst of irritation.

"We *are*," they said in unison, surprised that he thought they weren't.

"They started out and in three days they crossed seven mountains." Ty's eyes widened. So did Cedar's—their expression saying how impossible that really was. But no one spoke. "When they went down into the forest, they found that it was oddly familiar." Jacob turned to Cedar. "The cedar trees were huge and comforting." Cedar smiled, but tried to hide it, to seem as though she might be thinking of something else. "And they could see where Humbaba had walked in the forest."

"Footprints," said Soldier, as if he needed to explain.

Jacob nodded. "That night Gilgamesh grew afraid and had a dream that disturbed him. He dreamed three times, then wanted to go down the mountain. He took his ax and cut the first cedar. Humbaba heard it fall, and grew enraged. At that very moment Gilgamesh lost his strength, and fell into a deep sleep. When finally Enkidu woke him, his strength was much greater than before, and he acted like a man who was not afraid."

Ty looked out the window. If the sun had been out, or if it were just a little less rainy, he would have spent the afternoon with his friends in the schoolhouse, instead of in a room with

174

his sister and this strange grown man, and a heater he felt a
fascination for.

"Enkidu told Gilgamesh that the reason he wasn't afraid
was because he didn't know what was about to happen." Soldier shook his head in agreement, and Jacob wondered how
much of the story he understood, thinking, maybe, he understood it all.

"Humbaba came out," Ty paid attention, "and he was like
a raging bull. The Sun God sent the winds. Eight winds.
While the winds fought Humbaba, Gilgamesh and Enkidu
cut down seven cedars and stacked them. Humbaba threw
blazes at them, but each blaze died out before it hit. Finally
Humbaba was killed. Gilgamesh struck the first blow, Enkidu
the second, and Humbaba fell."

Soldier clapped, understanding this part more than the part
about the winds. He urged the children to join in, so they all
clapped and since Jacob was tired, he decided to make that the
end of the story.

"Is that all of it?" Cedar asked.

"For now."

"What else happens?" she urged. But Ty stood up and was
ready to go. Soldier was ready too. "Did they cut down all the
trees?"

"Enough to build a wall, and a temple, and a rampart."

"What's a rampart?" Ty. His first real interest.

"Something that protects you."

Cedar jumped off the bed, stumbling. "Ty. Look what you
did." She had knocked over the heater. Ty lifted it and moved
it across the room.

"What about Enkidu?" Soldier asked.

"Not now." Jacob pulled the covers up to his neck and
scooted down in the bed. Cedar kissed him good-bye. Ty did
too. Soldier shook Jacob's hand, but he seemed to want to kiss
instead, as the children had. Jacob noticed how Soldier had

175

trimmed his own hair and that one side was considerably closer cut than the other.

"We'll come tomorrow," Soldier told him, and he looked straight at Jacob, wishing for everything.

❆ A Shiny Black Lacquered Object

What Cedar and Ty thought of Soldier was what they had been taught to think. He could be liked, and trusted. He could be ridiculed in certain ways and in other ways he shouldn't be ridiculed at all. They learned early to show respect for Soldier, since he was older; but never to be friendly, or so friendly that he might start to come by the house and make a nuisance of himself.

So when Cedar and Ty saw him walking across a field or along a road, they wondered where he was going, his face so intent at those times. They knew that when he touched them, reached to touch their heads as he passed, that he reached into more than touch. He wished for so much, and his gaze did not deflect any of what he wished for. He was hard to look at straight on for that reason.

Once when the children followed Soldier to his apartment building, they hid behind trees as they followed. Soldier heard them giggling, scrambling along behind him and to the side of him in the brush. "Come on here," he called to them, and they came out from where they hid, and walked along with him. Later, they said he talked to them and asked questions as any adult might do.

When Oliver was twelve years old, he hid in the woods, hid in some trees behind Drue's house to watch a fire he knew he had started, and the man inside he knew he had hurt. But all these years he kept it to himself.

What he did know was this: he had dreamed so many times about a house, children, a quiet woman, an absent man. He dreamed it and called out in his dreams, though he couldn't remember the names when he woke. For even as he called, another woman came—the bulky-woman-figure. And she hit him, over and over. She was there, on him, and he could smell her. He cried out more some nights than others. The more he cried out, the more the heavy figure bore down on him. And he was tired, so tired.

As a boy, Oliver often went into houses after supper. People would be walking or visiting on porches, and Oliver would go into a house and take things—shiny or black lacquered objects. He kept each object for a few days, then returned it. Once he found a black wooden owl at Drue's house. It was his favorite treasure and he kept it for two weeks. The night he returned it, he saw as he walked in, a gun case beside the door. He had seen it before, the silky black guns that felt so cold he thought they must have been kept in the refrigerator. He picked one, as he had done before, and he wandered the house. When Drue walked in, it was too late for Oliver to run out, so he hid behind the sofa, crawling further toward the wall to kneel behind a chair.

He waited there, he didn't know how long, but a while, because Drue carried in wood and packed newspaper beneath it, then went to the kitchen to let water run and to put something on the stove. He came back into the room with a bowl of soup or stew, and Oliver could see from where he was the quick blaze catch as Drue lit the fire. A fine whoof went up. Oliver peeked to see, because he loved to watch his uncle light the fire at home. Then he shifted slightly to see better, but in doing so made a sound, not himself, but by pushing slightly against a chair. He tried to move into a more comfortable posi-

178

tion and when the chair scraped, Drue stood up. He spilled his stew. Oliver stood up and was afraid.

And though Oliver had not seen Mrs. Constant in five years, he had come to equate fear with the woman herself, and before he knew it he was back into his dream, seeing Constant above him, hearing her throat noises. And he heard too the sound the gun made as it went off in his hand, but the sound was in the dream that had come to his mind. He saw or remembered Constant, because she was the fear he felt here in front of Drue.

Drue had not said anything, but Oliver heard someone call a name. And he knew Drue was hurt, though Drue had not fallen. Drue's face turned an ashen color, his expression surprised, his eyes astonished.

Oliver still had the silky revolver in his hand, and in fact had been pushing the safety on and off (which he did not know was a safety). When Oliver hid behind the chair and Drue was in the kitchen, he pulled back the hammer and seeing it open, the inside of the gun a small mouth open, the tongue out, he looked down into it, closely, the way a doctor looks into a sick child's mouth. But this was before the chair scraped, before he stood up, before he entered his dream-fear-world of Constant, and heard the sound, and then saw Drue.

Drue's face kept its vigil, and he wavered though did not fall; so Oliver dropped the revolver onto the chair in front of him and ran to go out. He stumbled and pulled against the curtain beside him to catch himself. He pulled it halfway down so that the hem of the curtain flew into the fireplace. That was the start of it. The curtain catching, blazing up one side of the window and across the heavy valance, catching everything from then on.

When he was outside, Oliver still didn't run home, but stayed in the woods out back. He saw Callie (though he didn't know her name at the time) come to the house through the woods. And she went in the front door and dragged out Drue

179

wrapped in a rug, so that Oliver walked around to where she was, and said, "I *did* this. *I* did this." She was busy with the dragging, but she stopped to hear his words.

Callie knew he had done it, and she was glad in a way, because she had already seen Jake run away from the house. Then in those moments of dragging and deciding what to do, she saw this young boy trapped by one act that might change his life, and knew how that could happen. She felt he had already suffered enough, so she decided to cover it for him. She said, "Go home now, Oliver," and Oliver looked surprised to hear her say his name, but not too surprised because most of the town seemed to know it, though he couldn't remember theirs.

Later that night, when Oliver talked to Callie and the Judge, and his own uncle who came to take care of Drue, he tried to tell what happened. And he would get his dream mixed in to what he told, so that he could never exactly explain.

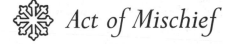 *Act of Mischief*

On his way to Locke's store, Jacob saw children on the street waiting for the school bus, their heads wrapped in heavy hats and scarves, their voices vociferous as a group of starlings. This was their last day of school before Christmas vacation; this was Jacob's last day in Sweetwater. Tomorrow he would leave for Virginia, but first he wanted to see Callie again, to say good-bye.

The store was not yet open. It was early, the morning not too cold, but cold for Tennessee. The mist, still thick, pulled up like tissue. Jacob could see through the store window that someone worked in the back, straightening. He turned again to see the children, but they were gone. The bus pulled away. He was startled when he heard the door unlock, and saw Mr. Brown.

Cecil Brown bought this store ten years ago though he never changed the name. People would call it Locke's anyway and would never call it Brown's, so he kept the name and the customers and a bowl of horehound candy at the register to keep people coming back. "Sorry, Jake, I startled you."

"No, no. I just walked up. Cedar and Ty got on the bus." Jacob pointed in the direction the bus had gone, but Mr. Brown didn't look. He saw it every day.

"Well, help yourself." He pointed to a pot of coffee on a table between two chairs. A round braid rug lay in front of the

181

chairs—a small oasis where people could come in, sit and talk, have coffee and buns in the morning, packaged cake in the afternoon. Mr. Brown opened a double package of cinnamon buns. Jacob took one. They were free.

The store looked very much the way it did when Callie and Ruben owned it. Ruben ran it for thirty years, Callie helped at the register. Now, Mr. Brown hired girls to help. The girl he had was Jewel. She came in and tied a white apron around her dress, then helped herself to a bun and poured coffee for each of them.

Two men walked in and Jacob recognized them as the men who talked to Soldier. They were the ones who took him to the field. When they came in, Jacob stood where they could see him.

Neither saw him at first, but went back to help themselves to coffee and buns. Then they would buy something, because if you came in and helped yourself you were expected to buy before leaving. And if normal courtesy was forgotten, Mr. Brown reminded, saying, "I got in some of those apples you like, Sammy, Vester." And they would buy some apples and maybe one other thing.

Vester was the older man and he saw Jacob first. He didn't speak, but nodded, checking friendliness. If he had done anything else, said something, nodded even a little differently, Jacob would have been set off and the whole scene would not have been peaceful. But he nodded, and Jacob nodded back; though it wasn't friendly. It was one quick nod, like a head bounce.

Sammy didn't see Jacob and said, "Vester, come on and sit down. We got time." Sammy settled into the chair draped with a chenille bedspread the color of raspberries. Women and young children perused the store carrying large baskets.

Jacob walked straight to Vester and said something low, so no one could hear. But Sammy heard and stood up, said "Sure," and he started to leave. Vester waited, not wanting to put down his cinnamon bun that he had taken only one bite out of.

"Wait a minute. Just a goddamn minute," Vester said to Sammy, as though Sammy were making him leave. And it seemed again that maybe the scene would not end peacefully.

Mr. Brown stood behind the meat counter trying to guess what kind of meat one woman wanted. She couldn't decide. She finally said, "Pork butt," and Jacob leaned and said something else inaudible. Vester left, but took the bun with him.

"There's some nice apples," Jewel called as she saw them go toward the door, but neither man turned around. Mr. Brown complained to the woman about the manners of some people, and said he didn't know how he could keep up the coffee and buns if people kept doing this. So the woman ordered two nice-size roasts along with the pork. Mr. Brown cut them both a little larger than usual for her.

Jacob sat in the raspberry-colored chair. The store was still dark, though the sunlight was beginning to enter it. And he could see in the back corner an old wood stove with its chimney going up through the ceiling like an elbow. They kept it for children to see. But Jacob remembered standing beside it, and Callie saying, "Not too close, Jake. You'll burn."

It was then that he heard of Callie's death.

A phone call told Mr. Brown and Mr. Brown told Jacob. They were the only ones in the store by then, though after a few moments someone else came in. A fat woman. And she heard only the last part and kept asking "Who?" and "What?," so Mr. Brown told it again from the beginning and Jacob listened this second time, closely or more closely than he listened the first. And when Mr. Brown was through telling it the second time, Jacob stood up and left.

He hurried toward the door as though he could do something to help, if he hurried. But the only place he hurried was

183

to Annie's house, and he handed her the few groceries she asked him to get, but that he had forgotten to pay for. He said that Callie was found, as though she were a child who had been lost.

Annie asked, "How?"

"She was found on the road. She left her house, must have known she was leaving for good, because she had her satchel of scarves with her, and she wore her lace-trimmed dress. She fell in a spot where evidently she had stopped or paused, looked up to see a bird or a piece of cloud. Her head, they said, looked as though it had been pulled back and something had made her fall backward, though no one was around." (Jacob hoped she had looked up to see some final vision she wanted to see all her life.) "But there was no hint in her expression as to whether what she saw frightened or relieved."

"Maybe," said Annie, "maybe she looked up to feel the wind." Then she asked, "Where? What road?" as though if she knew the road, she might know whether or not it was the wind that turned up Callie's head.

"The main road. They found her near the Johnsons'."

There were two main roads Callie could have taken from her house. One went beside the river and was the shortest route to town. It was the road she took when she came in to Sophie's and Ned's. At one time the road had been paved, but now the pavement was crumbled, plowed by long rows and patches of grass that had broken through the crust. And though it was no longer the main road and hadn't been for years, it was the road she chose. This road went straight through Garr's woods.

Annie put away the few groceries. Jacob went outside.

He walked to the place where he had seen the cowbone. He had meant to visit Callie again. When he stopped, Annie could see him from the window and called to him. "Jake? You all right?" He raised one hand to let her know he was. He wouldn't leave tomorrow as he planned. He knew that. He knew, too, that something had ended, more than Callie.

Jacob stood in this field like a farmer on market day when the night before there was a hailstorm that left ninety acres of his crop destroyed, another ninety damaged—a hailstorm that comes in twenty minutes on a hot night. Changes everything. The newspaper takes pictures of the man standing in the ruined field. People come. So he looks down to those plants that two days ago were lush and ready for picking, but now are flattened and torn. But the farmer doesn't answer the questions asked, "What will you do now?" or "Are you sorry you didn't harvest last week?" He looks to his ruined work and finds in the soil the ability to yield again, and in himself that same ability. So the photographer gets the picture, but there is not a picture taken of the farmer six-and-a-half months later, standing in a full-grown field, ready to plow. Hoping the hailstorm will not take his work again this year.

Annie called to Jacob again, but he didn't respond. His shoulders sloped along a line that ran from his head to his feet and made him look similar to the tall sunflowers that could edge an autumn field. As Annie looked out the window, she thought of Jacob, Albert, Verna, herself, and everyone she knew.

The people of Sweetwater bought Callie the finest casket —aluminum gray with gray-white satin lining and a tiny, delicate pillow that was also satin and held the faintest tinge of pink. At the end of the casket (for only a little extra) were the coveted embossed angels that sat among flowers that were also aluminum gray. The angels and the flowers rose up to a height of two inches.

The casket lay open. Callie's hair was curled in a way that Jacob had never seen it, and her clothes draped around her so that she looked more like she was covered than dressed. They had taken off her long dress and put someone else's clothes on her. That was what they had done. Jacob asked where her long dress was and they gave it to him.

That night Jacob spoke to Annie. "Would you help me with something?" he asked. The idea of Callie in that casket was unthinkable.

Annie, usually willing to help with anything, said doubtfully, "What?"

"We'll need to move her," Jacob said.

"Move Callie?" Annie thought Jacob meant to take her to a different cemetery.

"We need to put her into something," he looked at Annie's face, "more appropriate."

"Put her in what?" Her question implied that she would help, which she had not meant to imply.

"I already have something."

She knew he would do it. Would do it by himself if she didn't help. "How?"

He explained how he had been to the funeral home, asked the director to close the casket, seal it. Then he looked to see how he could get into a back window. "We can go tonight," Jacob told her. "You and Albert and me."

"Albert?"

"He's already agreed."

"Oh."

"I'll climb in a back window and then you and Albert can bring in the box I have. A plain box. It's maplewood, I've lined it with blankets from her house." Then his voice took on an impertinence he had in boyhood when he said, "We'll put her in it."

So they did. Jacob, Annie, and Albert in a borrowed station wagon took the maplewood box into the funeral home. They unsealed the gray aluminum casket and lifted Callie from the folds of satin cloth, placing her down in a way that made

186

Annie cry out slightly, a breath-cry, because Callie lay stiffer than Annie imagined her to be, and was so much heavier.

To Jacob, Callie's eyes seemed as though they might open to the blue they used to be (not the blue they were when he saw her a few weeks ago, that blue-streaked-with-white blue like the marble they always played for), but the blue that maybe she reflected when she turned up her head.

Annie and Jacob lifted most of the weight, though Albert helped by propping much of it onto the arms of his wheelchair. They loaded it into the station wagon and Jacob returned to reseal the empty casket. By then it was two a.m.

"What time is it?" Annie asked.

"We have time," said Jacob.

So Annie knew there would be more, that now they would bury her. She wondered where it would be. Jacob had already chosen a place, she was sure. His need to do this was so pressing that she had not questioned it too much, but followed it. But the idea of being here at night (changing Callie's body from one casket to another, burying her in some secret place) seemed almost beyond anything she believed she might do. She wondered if they could be arrested and decided they could. She tried not to think about what they did, but only to do it. Albert encouraged Jacob, not thinking about it either.

But it wasn't until they had taken the maplewood coffin out of the station wagon and laid it on the ground in the woods (where Jacob had dug a place and rigged a pulley of ropes to lower it), it wasn't until then that Jacob turned to Annie and Albert, the maplewood box deep in the ground, the ropes already thrown in, and he said, "I loved him, you know." Annie didn't know what he meant, thinking at first that he loved Callie and had made an error in his pronouns. But it wasn't that. And she knew then that it had to do with Drue, more than Callie, that in Jacob's mind the one he had moved, had saved from something, was Drue. And she said how we do these

187

things later that we wish we had done; but we do it for someone else, so that the regret is greater, but the relief comes anyway, because at least it was done, and someone was saved from something.

What he wanted to do was this: he wanted to be again in that house, Drue's. And to decide then to move the body out, to wrap it in the rug and pull it out as Callie had done. So now he did it for her, paying back in some way something he owed. But what he wished, really wished, was to step back and do over that one thing.

"I know you did," Albert told him, and Jacob could feel the sting and strain of his eyes against the welling up that would abundantly run down onto his shirt and jacket.

Jacob was glad they had put her other dress on her.

They had had trouble slipping her arms into those narrow sleeves, and had wondered how the coroner dressed a cadaver, finally having to forget that it was Callie, because Annie kept saying, "I can't do this. I can't," as Callie's arms would flop and fold, even in their stiffness. But in the end, it was Annie who stuffed the arms through to the tiny hole for the wrist, and it was Annie who buttoned most of the small buttons along her back.

They buried her next to the tree in Garr's woods.

There was no headstone, but the tree itself. The large headstone bought by the town was placed over the empty gray aluminum casket. It said

CALLIE BELDEN LOCKE: A LONG LIFE
April 24, 1888 Died December 20, 1984

Jacob hurried to fill the hole with dirt. It was almost daylight. And when they left, they left quickly, as if they were children who might be caught in their worst act of mischief.

188

 *Told Two Things*

The church was full, packed. People stood in the aisles, children scattered themselves on the floor. Cedar and Ty sat near the front with Verna. They were dressed up and fidgety, and wanted to get it over with. They had not known Callie in any way except as a strange, fanatic woman who lived in the woods, and whom people seldom saw. Though Ty knew her better than Cedar did.

There were men and women there who had known Callie when she was young, when Ruben was alive. No one knew her very well. Jacob thought it strange that people visited Callie in death, but wouldn't visit her in life. He guessed they hoped to have some of her longevity rub off on them—by attending her funeral, maybe her secret would be transmitted. Or else, he thought, the fact that she lived almost a hundred years gave the town a certain status ("Is that the town where the woman lives in the forest house?"), so people wanted to say they had gone to the funeral.

The organ was new and the person playing it had not practiced sufficiently, so there were many wrong notes which people tried to cover with their own voices; but they were unable to do so because their own voices slid into that ungainly note hit by the organist. The whole church full of people hit, throughout "Amazing Grace," notes of such discordance that the children put their hands to their mouths and giggled into

189

them, bending over, closing their eyes so no one would see. And before the song was over, even some of the adults smiled at the wretched notes the organist caused everyone to sing. And there were moments when everyone forgot this was a funeral. One more song was played, "There is a Happy Land." It went somewhat better. The children knew this one, so they sang it. It was not a song in the hymnbook, but one typed out (passed down from who knows where) and glued into the back of each hymnal. It was sung at special times—funerals, Easter, and was a favorite.

The preacher got up, approached the pulpit and propped the heels of his hands on either side. "Callie Belden Locke," he began, and people realized they had never known or else had forgotten she was a Belden, thinking only of her as Callie and how she was when she was old. "Married to Ruben Locke and for so many years a part of this town, of Locke's Store." He stammered a little. "In her early years she taught school." People squirmed. The preacher lowered his head. "Her life was full of hardship." No one looked at each other. "And I think that the hardest trial for her was in the way she was ignored." No one breathed. The children, sensing something more silent than just listening, turned around, strained to see if maybe somebody or something had come in which they didn't know about. "So here we've come to honor her." They breathed now. The children stopped looking. "To honor her now as she was not honored before," he looked to Jacob, "except by Sarah and Karl and their family, by Jacob who came back to be with her." Jacob felt a slight twinge at hearing his parents names called out, and hearing that he had come back to see Callie. People praised him for that, but all Jacob could think was what he had said to her—that he would be back, would see her again before he left. And now *she* had left, and he had not been back (though he had gone back once more during that same night).

190

"Will you be back?" she asked.

"Yes."

Callie told Jacob two things.

"There was more than the clipping tells. More that happened." And she told of the young boy who had done what he had not meant to do, as Jacob also did what he had not meant to do, but doing it. And the boy left, went into the woods. And as Jacob sat in this church which he had not seen in so many years, but in which he had sat as a boy, he saw the familiar way the light filtered in through the yellow stained-glass (all yellow glass, not different colored pictures as so many churches have, but all golden yellow), so that when the sun came through, it grew to be almost golden-like-fire against the dark red rug. And it had always been like that. As he noticed it, he remembered a frame of a boy standing at a window, looking in, his large sturdy face searching through a pane of glass that reflected the fire. And at the time, Jacob could not even tell it was a face, but saw only the fire; now it rose to his memory as a clod rises from the bottom of a pond—it loosens and rises to the top. So in remembering he knew it was a face, and knew whose face it was. He turned around to see if Soldier was here in the church. He turned all the way to look at the doorway, and he saw Soldier's large figure blocking the door as if he were the keeper of these people, a protector at the gates.

But Jacob saw Callie twice that night. When the dance was over and everyone went home, Jacob went home too with Annie and Albert. But he woke at two a.m. or three, and went back to Callie's house. He knocked and when she didn't answer, he walked in. The door was not locked. He could hear her calling from her bedroom. She sat up in bed, and talked in a loud voice. Her eyes were glazed, powdered almost. She's asleep, he thought, and she ranted babblings from a dream. But as he listened, her rantings seemed to come from more

191

than sleep or dream. The way her eyes asked for something from him indicated a plea.

So he sat with her all night, answering her at times in a calm voice. Sometimes she seemed to hear and lay back down. But once she saw something come toward her. She had been staring for a long while at the bedspread, then she lifted her head to look at the other side of the room. She drew back, suddenly, her whole body withdrawing from whatever she saw. And she yelled, so Jacob bent to pull her to him, hold her like a child and he hoped that what she saw was not him, and that he had not been the one to scare her. But she held onto him, still looking to the other side of the room, until something subsided and she went back to sleep. She was propped against Jacob's shoulder. When he laid her down, he noticed how her shoulders stuck up through her nightclothes like clothespins, her body ready to hang out to dry in a breeze. As she lay down, she breathed out and he thought that wood could be kindled by her hot breath, though her arms were colder than the covers.

All night she summoned people Jacob had never heard of, and some people Jacob had heard of, and once she summoned him. But she did so as if he were a small boy, saying "Jake? What are you doing now?" as though she had walked up on him while he was playing, or she said, "You look fine," as though he had asked how he looked. Then she woke and her voice was gravelly, though she didn't say anything but made only a noise. And the sound made Jacob feel as if a cold wind had blown through his clothes.

She got out of bed, rawboned, exhilarated, and paced back and forth reminding Jacob of an animal looking for its home. She was shuddering, oblivious to anything. Jacob knew not to touch her. She wore a man's nightshirt that came to her ankles and her feet stuck out beneath as in a humorous drawing.

When she came back to bed, she walked with an elegance

192

that ignored her nightshirt and her feet. Her arms hung loose from her shoulders. And it seemed to Jacob that she had gotten up merely to straighten a few things on a table or to get some water, neither of which she did. She smiled a little as she got back into bed and pulled the covers around her. Jacob smiled back, only slightly, for he could not be sure that anything deliberate (a touch, a smile) might not bring her into a state of mind that would be more difficult than this. She was that old. She had not lost her mind, but only went in and out of the past and present, and maybe some other place that Jacob had only read about. But whatever it was, her pacing, her sounds, it was like some dance or song that she heard only for herself.

Jacob watched her face in sleep. It fell slack, her cheeks falling onto themselves, and the next time she woke, she woke slowly. Jacob had dozed off, sitting in a chair next to her bed. But he heard her wake, even though it was before he was fully awake. He heard her stir and felt her hand on his arm. He sat upright not knowing what to expect, but saw that her expression was clear and her words reasonable when she asked, "What are you doing here?" and Jacob said, "I came back," and she said, "That's fine. You can stay," as though she were offering shelter to someone who had no other place to go.

She wanted to talk, her mind now lucid, so Jacob asked about Sarah, not asking directly. Callie answered what Sarah had told her, the way Sarah told it. And though Jacob had no way of knowing what she would tell, had never heard this before, he knew *This is what I have come to hear.*

"At eight years of age," Callie said, "your mother let her youngest brother drown while she bathed him. She bathed him each morning during the summer, while her mother was in the garden." And Callie told him in the exact words that Sarah used to tell her.

"'And it came to me while washing him,' Sarah told me, 'that if my hand slipped beneath that sweet neck that his head

193

would fall back and might go beneath the water. And how dangerous that would be. But I don't remember doing it. I just remember thinking what would happen if I did. And I took him out of the washtub and wrapped him in a towel on the floor. I dried him carefully. And because of his stillness I could dress him without trouble. He had stopped his screaming finally. Mother was in the garden.'

"'You still have Buddy in that tub?' Sarah's mother called in. 'Take him out now. He'll shrivel.'

"'He's out,' Sarah called back. And she had him nearly dressed in what he would be buried in. 'I put him in the crib,' Sarah told me, 'and laid a full bottle in there beside him. It was juice, not milk, for he was still nursing. It was an hour before anyone checked. Mother screamed when she found him. I screamed too, because he looked so different than when I laid him down. He'd gotten fat and blue.'

"And Sarah always stopped for a full minute before going on," Callie said, and she leaned toward Jacob, her face as close to his as a lover's. "Then she would say, 'They never accused me,' or sometimes she said, 'They never asked if I had done it. But they knew it happened while I bathed him, because the autopsy showed the lungs full of water.'"

Callie shifted away from Jacob. Jacob stayed still. "She told me and as she told me she would remember it again and her eyes would close off and she'd say, 'And I held up his head and I remember letting the neck go, seeing that small head bob without fight or struggle. Nothing. Like being inside the womb again. Because Mother explained to me that a fetus lived in water like a fish and how it would be difficult to enter this world and they would have to hit his back to make him breathe. And I remember thinking how he must like being in that again, because he had been screaming and now he didn't scream at all. But I didn't know you couldn't go back.'

"And Sarah told me this story over and over through the years of our friendship. I would say, 'It's all right, Sarah. It doesn't matter now.' But one day I said, 'That's enough. You don't have to say it again,' and Sarah nodded. After that she didn't tell the story, and she never told Karl that I know of. And though people mentioned it, they never mentioned it to her, or to Karl."

Now, as Jacob thought of it, he saw what Callie meant to tell, though she told it finally in this story of his mother instead of in her effort to relieve him.

Something was passed down, he thought. A legacy, perhaps. Or maybe from Sarah's mother and father, who lived in the time of the Civil War, a commonplace killing of brothers. Or passed from Cain and Abel, borne through thousands of years, the burden immigrating from other lands.

And suddenly, it did not matter that his own courage had failed. Sitting here in this yellow-stained church, the children sitting cross-legged on the floor, giggling into their own hands, unable to be sad, he saw it did not matter that his mother let go that baby's head to return to the watered sounds. It did not matter that Jacob had run. It did not matter either that he had lost his own son, who died for no reason at all on a spring morning when the sun broke through brighter than it had in months and warmed the buds in the ground, but could not warm Jacob who accepted with great bitterness this loss. It did not matter that two cruel men took one good man to a field for sodomy and mawkish laughter.

What mattered here in this place, what mattered here on this day, not bright and warm, but covered with an early sodden light, was that all of this was but a subterranean rhythm. Something to be forgiven, consoled.

For people treated each other in horrid ways, both loving and horrid; but being disappointed finally in who they are. They try for their lifetime to do anything to keep from knowing that who they are does not measure up to the image they hoped to project; but may, in fact, be closer to the image they have spent their lifetime criticizing and abhorring. So that now

each man abhors himself, or else must learn to love those he
has failed to love.

The service was over.

On the way to the graveyard, Jacob, Annie, and Albert rode
in the first car behind the hearse. Verna, Cedar and Ty rode
in the second car. Not many people came to the gravesite, but
still there were almost twenty gathered around when the
preacher arrived and gave a benediction.

Cedar and Ty said they didn't want to get out of the car, but
then they did; and stood in front next to the preacher. Cedar
even hurried toward the grave, wanting to get there first.

When everyone left, Jacob stayed. Annie left her car for
him, and she and Albert rode home with Verna. Jacob walked
to the posterns that formed a gateway out of the cemetery and
into the forest. It was not the forest where Callie was buried,
but Jacob pretended it was. The forest was heavy with fog that
had not yet burned off, even though it was almost noon. Jacob
was tired. He walked into the fog until he could not see the
things around him. He wished for light. He could see those
things which were very near, and though the sun was far from
setting, the light did not reach in here. And this fog seemed
to carry a light of its own, only different.

"Sometimes we went to that dry tree at the edge of Garr's
woods," Callie told Jacob the night he came back. "It had
grown taller," she raised her arm to indicate tallness. "But the
marks left by the ax grew wider, not higher, and the bark had
split or broken off in places through the years. But the height
had not been affected by that early ax." Then she spoke of it
as she might speak of an old friend. "That dry tree," she said,
"that dry tree bore the marks for us. Ruben and me. We would
go there and sit."

It would be the last thing she told him that night, though
she had told him so much more. "It taught me something, I
think. But it may not be something you want to learn."

196

As Jacob came out of the forest, the fog had moved over the ground, had swallowed the church, the hill, and the grave-diggers already packing the dirt with their shovels. They buried the empty casket, silk pillow and satin-lined interior. When they saw Jacob, they looked startled as if they were young boys doing the very thing they had always been told not to do.

On the way to his car, Jacob saw Soldier dressed in his Sunday suit and his jacket delivering papers on a bike.

"Where'd you get the bike?" Jacob yelled to him.

Soldier veered to the curb and came to a stop. "Mr. Brown and some others bought it for me. You like it?" He pointed to the large basket behind the seat that held his papers.

Jacob said he liked it and commented on its red color. "Are you almost through?" he asked, meaning the delivery of papers.

"No." He brushed off his coat and Jacob saw the place at the shoulder that was still torn.

"Why don't you come by Annie's house tonight," Jacob pointed to his own shoulder. "We'll get that coat sewn up for you."

Soldier nodded then said, "And maybe you can come to the cave tomorrow?"

"What?" Jacob had forgotten, but pretended he remembered. "Yes," he told Soldier.

He had planned to leave tomorrow, but changed his plan. He would call Molly and tell her he wouldn't be home until Saturday. "We'll call Cedar and Ty," he added, "They can go with us."

That night Annie sewed up Soldier's coat and gave him a large piece of pie. She noticed that he carried a Save the Snail Darter button in his pocket, and she asked him about it. When Soldier left, he thanked Annie, and Annie commented on how sometimes Soldier said things that didn't seem retarded at all.

197

✻ The Moon and Its Three Children

It was later that same night when Jacob stopped by Verna's house. He wanted to tell her what time he would come by the next morning. Verna and the children had been Christmas shopping, but the children were in bed.

"Soldier wants to take us to the cave," Jacob told Verna. "It seemed important to him."

"I know." Verna had the new baby in a small bed near her in the kitchen. Jacob leaned again to see the face. "He's got a job out there on weekends," Verna said. "He's a guide." She got up to check on the baby. "He came by here tonight."

"He came out here?" It was not a question so much as a repetition of what Verna had said. Jacob thought nothing of it until Verna lifted her head to the window.

"He does sometimes, then, before he goes home, he likes to walk around back there." She pointed toward the field, the barn.

Jacob turned to the window. It was dark, though the glow from town left a thin strip of light along the horizon. "Is he out there now?" Jacob asked.

Verna sliced some bread and dunked it into her coffee. She offered Jacob a piece. Jacob waved off the bread, but asked for coffee. "He went out there about ten minutes ago," Verna said.

Verna's kitchen was large. There was room for a sofa beside the refrigerator. On the wall were two pictures: one of four

198

birds flying into a heavy winter morning and on the ground some hunters with their guns poised; the other, a mountain stream that flowed into a lake that could be seen partially at the corner of the picture. Jacob stared at the pictures and talked a few minutes, then left. He said, "I'll see if Soldier's still out there." He pointed toward the field. "Maybe he'd like a ride home."

"That'd be nice." Verna closed the screen door behind Jacob and hooked the small hook-latch. She closed the other door, but didn't lock it.

As Jacob neared the dark out-buildings, he called. No one answered. He felt pulled toward the barn as if by a rope, and he thought *I don't want to know what I will know, already know.* But still he was drawn. *I don't want to go here, see this.* And he called "Soldier?" No answer. "Oliver?" he called.

Then Jacob saw Oliver, silhouetted against the sky and the town's light. He could see him through the open ends of the barn. The figure he saw leaned against the back of a cow. Oliver stood on something, a milking stool. Also silhouetted was a harness hanging from a high board and a piece of broken plow that stuck up beside the door like an odd winter bush. He could see nothing of the barn, the barn itself being too dark; but he saw what was darkened against the light from the town's sky. The barn itself was a large hollow sanctuary, palpitant with its own sounds, and keeping behind it a numinous quality reiterative of his second sleep.

Jacob did not call again, but saw in that deep light how Oliver moved. And he thought at first that Oliver had hung himself, seeing the harness hanging like a dead rope and the milking stool that Oliver stood on. But then Oliver moved, not suddenly, but slowly sliding downward, softly, to hide at the side of the cow. He hid from Jacob's voice.

So Jacob left as though he had not found Oliver, had looked for him but not found him. It took only a brief moment to take

199

in the figure, the harness, the plow, the soft sliding down to kneel or hide. But in that moment Jacob had seen someone's loneliest urge. And he wondered if this is what they demanded of Oliver—to be as lonely as this? Was it what they demanded of each other?

The two men had taken Oliver to the field. They shamed and embarrassed him. They showed him how alone he was. Oliver had not known until they came, showed him. His uncle had tried to shelter, but that night those men taught him. They didn't know that what would be learned would be for Oliver a help, his way of life.

It was not that night that taught him, but what happened in all the nights after that. Because Oliver found himself often in the farthest barn off the road to Verna's, where one cow always was. And he had been shown how, had been told it was like a woman. And he was told never to take a woman. He never had. But here, it wouldn't hurt anybody. They taught him that and he learned it.

But even Oliver knew, when he stood in the mouth of that barn getting ready to go in, that the relief he would find here was not enough. But he didn't realize that nothing he ever did would be enough.

Jacob wondered what Oliver's face had been as he heard someone call him from outside, if his expression had been one of fear or shame. In that one moment, Jacob saw Oliver's head drop down, saw his body jerk once before moving so slowly to huddle in the hay-barn-smell. Jacob was sure Oliver had talked for a while to that cow, was sure that the night comforted him and that he would return from time to time to this place where now he knelt or sat, his arms heavy at his side, and his forehead leaning against the hot brown flank of the cow.

Before Jacob got to Annie's house, there was a downpour of rain, not like a winter rain, but an inexhaustible torrent that

200

poured as in warmer weather. It poured onto the fields, on Oliver's barn, and on Verna's half-locked house.

Jacob honked for Soldier at his apartment house, but the children stood in the yard when he drove up to Verna's at nine o'clock. Verna placed a picnic basket on the back seat and gave instruction about what to eat first and what not to eat first. She nodded to Soldier and said she hoped he had a good time. Ty got in back and Cedar climbed in front. Verna kissed them through the window.

"Have you ever been?" Soldier asked Jacob, referring to the cave.

"I went with Drue. Years ago."

"Who's Drue?" Ty asked, and there was a silence more intense than anything that might have been said.

"That was his brother." Cedar turned around to explain. "He burned in a fire." She looked to Jacob as though she wasn't sure. Jacob nodded that that was right, and he thought how Cedar had lost her brother too. On a winter pond. Her chin stuck out and she looked straight ahead, so Jacob decided not to mention it.

"I remember it," Soldier's voice came from the back seat, hollow and slow. "I remember that." He leaned forward in his seat, but didn't say more.

They followed signs that announced "Caverns Parking, Four Miles"; other signs that said "Underground Caves! A Guided Tour!" Near the entrance of the cave was a ticket lady in a booth.

"None of this was here," Jacob told them, and he made a sweeping gesture with his arm that indicated disgust.

Soldier took Jacob's statement with a sense of pride. "I work here on weekends," he told.

They bought tickets and walked into a narrow entrance that quickly became large on the inside. They looked up to see bats moving from one side to the other. Soldier told them one whole cave had been sealed off, because hundreds of bats congregated there.

The children had heard this before, but they listened as if being told for the first time. As Soldier talked, his voice grew clear, and he told in a memorized, though effective way, of how the Indians used the cave for a meeting place. Cherokee Indians. How in the Civil War there was mining equipment and the cave was used to make gunpowder. Soldier told them all this as they climbed into the boat and pushed off. Jacob took an oar and gave the children one, telling them to share it. Soldier sat in the back of the boat to guide it with his own oar. This job gave to Soldier's life a new latitude.

The children pointed to the cave that was sealed off. Cedar said she wanted to see it, Ty said he was glad it was sealed and told Cedar she was stupid. Cedar said to let her have the oar now, because he'd had it long enough.

The water inside the cave was both crystal clear and black. "One time," Soldier told them, "the water worked its way down to a low spot and a boy crawled through the place that was usually covered. When he did, he saw more water than anybody knew was here." He gestured with both arms. "Nobody knew there was a sea in here." He laughed and they rowed to the middle. "The boy told people in town, but when they came out, the water level had risen again. So no one believed him." Soldier loved to tell the story. In here, in this place, nothing Soldier said was distorted. "It was fifty years later that the Lost Sea was found." Then he added as he pointed to a passageway, "In there are the hidden chambers."

Jacob watched Soldier speak and saw a confidence and clarity that was not available to his everyday speech. Soldier practiced these words so well that, except for slight mispronunciations, he spoke in a normal way.

Cedar perched herself at the bow of the boat and looked like one of those heads of women at the front of a ship, one that might keep the sailors from harm. She gave the oar to Ty for a while, but said she wanted it right back. Jacob sat in the middle with Ty. As Soldier spoke, Ty bent over to put his hands in the water.

There were lights all around the walls, many lights, though the effect was one of candlelight. The water glimmered and left the impression of snakes moving over the top. They rowed toward the passageway.

"Mama won't bring us in here," Cedar said, her back a little arched. She said it as though now she understood why. They were going straight toward a passage that, as far as they could see, turned into darkness. "Are there any lights on in there?" Cedar asked.

"Yes," Soldier told her, but you couldn't tell if that were true. He told them the name of the passageway. It was something Indian sounding and none of them knew if Soldier had said it right.

They slid into the tunnel and grew quiet. Jacob felt himself open to the oblivion. Cedar climbed down closer to the middle of the boat and as she did the boat rocked slightly, each person having the thought that they might turn over and fall onto that surface that moved like hundreds of snakes. Cedar cried out, Ty gasped. Their echoes came back hollow and vexed.

As the walls closed in, the children reached to touch the stone, push it away. There were lights mounted high along the sides, but upon approaching a curve, if it was a sharp one, the light behind them could not provide enough to last until they rounded the curve and saw a light beyond. So that for a few moments they slid in darkness as thick as water, and it seemed to all of them that they were *in* the water, though not able to drown there. Then the light beyond would show, and though no one spoke at those times, when the light did appear either Cedar or Ty said what it was they could see. And sometimes it was the same thing they had seen before, but they repeated it, because no one wanted to mention the complete joy felt at seeing the light there, or the lack of purpose felt in those lightless moments.

"You never finished that story." It was Cedar. She wanted to hear a voice. "Tell us the rest of it."

"Well," said Jacob. "Enkidu dies."

"How?" The voice Soldier's. He couldn't help bumping the sides of the narrow passage, so he pushed now with both arms to position the boat in the middle again. No one else was working.

"He was wounded by Humbaba. Then later by the Bull of Heaven."

Ty wanted to know about the Bull of Heaven, so did Soldier; but Jacob said that Gilgamesh had had a lot of adventures, and that they wouldn't have time to hear them all. Ty reached long with his foot and kicked the seat in front of him.

"Before Enkidu died he said how furious he was."

"I would be too," Soldier tells.

"And he remembered his life in the Steppe, the woods. 'Everything had life to me,' Enkidu told Gilgamesh, but Enkidu was almost dead even as he said this: 'Everything had life to me, the sky, the storm, the earth, water, wandering, the moon and its three children, salt, even my hand had life. It's gone. It's gone.' And Enkidu wished that he had never had a man's life. Just to have it, then lose it seemed cruel. Then he looked at Gilgamesh, who must stay alive, who would experience loss and know how it is to be left alone. 'You will have to wander alone,' Enkidu told him."

"I know that," Soldier said, as though it had been said to him, not this time, but some time in the past. Soldier often spoke when no one expected, because he spoke whatever he felt at exactly the moment he felt it.

"Enkidu told Gilgamesh that he would wander looking for a life that's gone, or a life that he would have to find for himself."

Soldier said, "The moon and its three children." It was the

phrase he remembered from what Jacob had just told. And Jacob knew as Soldier said it that he applied the image to the four of them sitting in the boat. But he didn't know which of them were the three children and wondered if Soldier considered himself the moon.

"So Gilgamesh understood how death comes to everybody. He planned a journey, a wandering that he hoped would bring Enkidu back to life, and find some kind of everlasting life for himself."

"Can he do that?" Soldier.

"No." Jacob. "At first he thought he could bring back his brother just by weeping, but then he heard of one who had life without any fear of death—Utnapishtim—a man who would never die. Gilgamesh decided to find him and ask his secret."

"Where is he *now*?" Cedar.

"Who?"

"The man who never dies."

Jacob hadn't thought of the possibility of Utnapishtim still being alive, but Cedar had bought the story so completely that she believed now in a life without death and all of it. "He must be in the place far off, where he was when Gilgamesh found him."

"He found him?"

"Yes. He found Utnapishtim the Faraway—that was his name. He had built a boat and survived the flood."

"That was Noah." Ty, showing off Sunday School lessons.

"Not in this story. Gilgamesh, though, had to go through a mountain to reach Utnapishtim. He was warned, because no one had ever done this. The journey had twelve leagues of darkness."

"*I* know how long a *league* is," said Cedar, but she didn't tell and no one asked.

"It's dark in here too," Soldier said, focusing on Gilgamesh and his journey.

"Yes," said Jacob, "like this. It was so dark that after only

205

two leagues Gilgamesh looked before him and behind him and there was no light. After four leagues the darkness was thick and there was no light. He couldn't see anything before him and nothing behind him. At the end of six leagues of darkness the air was still thick and there was no light, and he could see nothing ahead and nothing behind. When he had gone eight leagues Gilgamesh cried out, because he could see no light, nothing before him nor behind. He felt blind. After ten leagues the sun streamed out. The Sun God spoke to Gilgamesh and said, 'You will not find the life you are looking for.' Gilgamesh didn't believe him though, because he had already come so far."

"When does he find Utnapishtim?" Soldier had tried to pronounce the name.

"First, he had to cross water with a ferryman. This journey lasted only three days, but seemed much longer. The ferryman guided him until finally Gilgamesh arrived at the place where Utnapishtim lived. Gilgamesh told how he wanted to find life without dying.

"It was then that Utnapishtim told the story of the Flood and how the gods decided to let him live forever, but he didn't really know why they chose him. He told Gilgamesh to stay awake for six days and seven nights, but no sooner had he made that suggestion did Gilgamesh fall asleep. Utnapishtim said to his wife, 'Look at him. He wants Life Forever and he can't even stay awake for a little while.' But the wife had pity and suggested they wake him. 'No,' Utnapishtim said, and he told his wife to bake loaves of bread: one loaf for each day that Gilgamesh slept. She did this and put them beside his head.

"When Gilgamesh woke there were seven loaves of bread beside him. The closest loaf was still warm, the first one baked was covered with mold. Utnapishtim told Gilgamesh to count the loaves he had failed to eat and he would know how many days he had missed by sleeping.

Gilgamesh was sorry and asked what he should do. 'Bathe,

change clothes, and go back home,' Utnapishtim told him. But before Gilgamesh left, Utnapishtim (because of his wife's urgings) told Gilgamesh a secret. 'There is a plant that grows underwater. It has a prickle and a thorn, like a rose,' he told, 'and if you take it, it will restore your youth.'

"How *long* is this story?" Ty asked, not even vaguely concerned with preserving his youth.

"Shhh." Soldier. The only one who knew what that plant could do.

"Gilgamesh tied heavy stones to his feet and jumped into the water bed. He found the plant and decided to take it to the old men of his town, but also to save some for himself. But before he got home, he stopped for water at a well, and when he bent down a snake smelled the plant's sweetness and snatched it away. The snake sloughed his skin."

"He didn't get anything he went after," Cedar said. She wanted a better ending.

"That's just what Gilgamesh said," Jacob told her, "He said to the ferryman 'Why have I done all this? I have done all of this for nothing.' Then he returned home to his friends."

They all looked so disappointed that Jacob added, "Well, but he lived for a long time, and when he died people remembered him as someone wise and strong, a builder who brought us the tale of the Flood. He wrote down stories for us, wrote them on a stone."

"That was good." Soldier.

"Yeah." Ty. "But it was *long*."

Cedar was silent, still thinking.

They came to a place in the tunnel where the lights stopped, and they could see that the tunnel did not stop, only the lights. Jacob said, "You want to go farther?"

Ty said nothing, neither did Cedar, so Soldier pulled the boat toward that place where the air looked as dark as the stone.

They proceeded as blind people in a boat, bumping into the

wall. Ty hunched over as far as he could, so did Cedar, and Jacob. Though none of them knew the other was hunched. The only sound was their breathing and the water that lapped and sucked louder than before.

"That's far enough," Cedar said, and Jacob knew it was always the woman who decided that. All his life. So he trusted her words, that voice young as it was. And when she spoke, it came from both in front of and behind them, and to Soldier it too seemed a good place to stop. They didn't row backward or forward. Then Soldier said, "Jake?" and Jacob waited a moment before he answered.

"What, Soldier?"

"It was on a Sunday night."

"What?" And though they were speaking in a normal way, it was as though they had reverted to a time preverbal.

"Sunday night. I came in. I hid." He told it all in the best way he could, losing his practiced speech, but telling how he hid himself behind the chair then stood up and there was Drue. "And I had a gun," he told this part the way he told it that night to Callie, his uncle, the Judge. "And I remember I had a gun," then he went into his dream-remembering, "but I heard it go off, something, but I did not know what it was. But it was me doing it. Callie, the Judge, my uncle, they told me. They told me not to tell, so I did not. But I asked Callie if I could tell you. A few months ago, I asked. She said I could tell one person. You."

Jacob at this point knew he should say something. "I knew it was you," he told him. "Yesterday at Callie's funeral when I turned around and saw you. I knew then. But not until then." Then he added, "It was the way you were standing, or something, your face. I remembered that you looked in through the window that night. It was your face, though younger."

"Callie said you ran," Soldier told him. "I ran too." He didn't know how to explain it. "And so," he began again, repeating the incident as though the first time were practice, or as though it had gone through his own head so many times in this repetitious way, that as it came out, it would also have to be repeated.

As Soldier spoke, Jacob looked before them and behind them and there was no light. Soldier spoke on until Jacob wished he would stop, wanted to tell him he would not find the life he was looking for. But Soldier already knew that, so maybe Soldier was telling Jacob. When Jacob thought about it, he felt calm—and that calmness felt the same as loving someone.

Soldier finished his telling and Jacob knew there was nothing adequate he could say to him. Any response he thought of wasn't enough, so he said, "I know, Soldier. I know how you feel." And though no one could see, they could hear Soldier make odd sounds. Then Soldier suggested they go back out and when he spoke Jacob knew it was not sadness that made those sounds, because when Soldier suggested they go back out, his voice was strong, not broken, and he spoke to Jacob with the kinship of an ordinary man. The boat floated out of the passageway, and they could see now the beginnings of light.

The response *had* been enough, Jacob thought, because the way to lessen pain was to share another's. His mother had known this, so had Callie. Judge Bradford and Doc. Now Jacob knew it, and Soldier. "It's all right," he told Soldier, and when he said it, he forgave himself.

The children sat unusually quiet. They didn't understand exactly what had been told, but knew that Soldier's tone of voice deserved the respect of not being interrupted. Now they began to argue over which oar to use, though they couldn't even see the oars. Jacob told them to stop and they stopped. Soldier backed out the boat toward the light. "There. There it is," he said, and paddled harder.

As they slid out of the dark hollow, Jacob could see the emergence of the three figures, knowing he too emerged. But they were not looking at each other, nor did they look at Jacob.

Soldier was stooped in his working like a weary beast. The two children flanked him and in the flatness of that scene (because of partial light), they seemed a picture on a wall far from Jacob. But as they slid into a more open space of the cave, everyone took on his own roundness of position. And as they went across the smooth lake, the children slowly regained their voices, though not to argue.

"Are you cold?" Cedar asked Ty. Ty held his arms tightly against his chest. "You want my coat?" Cedar removed her coat and told Ty to put it on. She held it for him so he could get his arms in. The warmth was immediate, and Ty smiled. They were glad to see again the wide expanse of water. It looked as calm as a field. They crossed without much conversation and tied up the boat. Soldier helped everyone climb out, and though they already knew their way, Soldier wanted to direct them and enjoy as long as he could the privilege of his role.

Cedar's coat hung to Ty's knees and though she walked with her shoulders hunched a little, she didn't seem to feel the cold. In the car Jacob praised Cedar for giving her coat to Ty. She said she wasn't cold anyway. And they rode, all of them, in silence, an intense quiet as after a scare.

Jacob suggested they stop for ice cream, and they talked about what a good morning and afternoon they had had, and how much fun it would be to tell Verna. But just before they got home, Ty noticed the picnic basket in the back seat, and mentioned that they had forgotten to eat what Verna fixed. Jacob pulled off the side of the road and opened the basket to find that the food looked good, but they didn't want any of it. He unwrapped the sandwiches and threw one into the woods. A squirrel came to nibble. Cedar unwrapped her sandwich took one bite and threw it in a different direction. One bird flew down, but they couldn't see if the bird had found the bread. Ty did the same. And Soldier. So they flung food into the woods, enjoying the absurd freedom of the act. But they left the paper and two bananas in the basket.

Upon arriving home, Verna said, "Was the lunch good?" and they all nodded. She saw in the basket the trash and two bananas, and fussed because they hadn't used their napkins. Cedar had bitten once into her sandwich, so that she could say it was good. But then she added, "We shared it with the squirrels," and Verna said how nice that was.

Jacob took Soldier home.

"Thank you," Soldier told Jacob and Jacob said he was welcome. Soldier wanted to say more, looked as if he wanted to say something he didn't understand how to say.

"I'm glad you told me," Jacob said. "It's all right. I'm glad you said all that about Drue."

"Yes," said Soldier. "We are lucky."

Jacob couldn't figure the reason for Soldier saying this, but connected it to the time in the hospital when Jacob said he was "lucky," and Soldier had been confused so that now at a time when something difficult was over, he said it, "We are lucky," thinking that the difficult part was over and still they were here and not harmed too much.

"Yes." Jacob let Soldier out in front of the apartment house and said good-bye. He reached to shake Soldier's hand through the window and Soldier held it longer than Jacob meant for him to. Soldier's face hung at the window of the car, looking in for Jacob to tell him one more thing, and Jacob didn't know what that thing should be. But Soldier's face stayed and his hand held, wishing for a last word, so Jacob said again, "Yes, we *are* lucky," and it made no sense at the end of his telling good-bye, but it was what Soldier wished to hear, and Soldier brightened, as if he had been carrying something huge, the way an ant does in the hot sun going toward shade. So he let go of Jacob's hand and turned toward his apartment.

Jacob woke the next morning and felt a sudden excitement about going home. He missed Molly and would be glad to see her. The hard sunlight brought him into the day as it had done

211

in his childhood, but never since. (Except, he thought, when the woman you love gets up before you do and calls you to a breakfast that you smelled before she called. Then she sits on the bed and rubs you awake, your back and hair; and she smells like breakfast herself, so you tell her if you had a fork, she would be enough. So she hands you an old fork and falls in bed beside you, so that when you have your breakfast later, it is cold, but tastes better than any meal you have had in your life.)

 *Familiar Ground*

When Molly got up this morning, it was a bright Virginia day. The radio told her the temperature would rise to forty-six degrees. She planned to shop for groceries and make loaves of bread, a few desserts for the freezer. Christmas was less than a week off and Tom would be here with Mona, Stephanie and Paul. Stephanie was four last week, Paul five. It would be good to have children around. She would shop for a tree and have it put up when Jacob arrived. Maybe even decorated. She felt she could do anything today.

But Molly thought of Joseph this time of year. During the few weeks before Christmas, she thought of him constantly, each year remembering how old he would be, wondering what he might be doing. She would take out his picture and imagine how he had grown into a man. And though she rarely mentioned her thoughts to Jacob, she knew he did this too. For often during the few days before Christmas, Jacob would say, "Joseph used to like this, didn't he?" and point to a special sweet cinnamon bread she had made, or a dish of scalloped potatoes. And she would say, Yes, then later without referring to anything he would ask, "What do you think he would be?" and Molly would know exactly who he meant, and would answer "A scientist, maybe." Jacob liked her suggestion. And though Molly didn't think he dwelled on those early memories as much

213

as she did, she knew he wondered. But Molly found her own mind constantly going back to remember and wonder, and for those two weeks each year before Christmas, she had him in her mind more than any other time.

It was last year when Tom arrived for Christmas (with his wife and children) that he found his mother seated in an odd way at the end of her bed. She had not heard them come in, nor had she heard them call to her. Jacob wasn't home. She sat, facing the window and when Tom walked in he knew something was wrong.

His mother didn't look different, but she was paralyzed still as stone. She couldn't even call out, but only sat, so still, not looking tired or worn-out, but bright-eyed, willing herself to move. But her hands lay flat onto her thighs and gave the impression that they could not be released. Her head and mouth seemed on the verge of speaking.

"Mother?" Tom asked, as if he hated to disturb her if she might be resting or thinking. She didn't turn her head. "Mother?" His voice more urgent now, was quieter. He took hold of her shoulders and laid her back. As he did, it was as though he loosened, found oil for those joints and she came alive in front of him in much the same way you might imagine a large doll would come to life: slowly, moving the joints, testing, then not believing her movements at first.

"Oh, Tom," was all she said.

"How long have you been sitting like that?" His tone was admonitory.

"Not long." Her mouth didn't move exactly right when she talked, not everything coming back to life at once. "Tom," she said. Then she said, "Don't tell your father."

"Why?"

"It isn't the first time."

"Have you seen a doctor?"

214

"Don't have to. I know what it is."

When Tom asked What, she didn't answer.

"I want to see those 'churren'" she said, making fun of her pronunciation before Tom could. Tom never noticed how his mother pronounced things until he moved to Vermont. Molly guessed they pointed it out to him, so that he pointed it out to her. The difference was that Tom tried to change his own way of talking (as much as he could), and Molly had no intention of changing hers.

"Churren?" she called. She had almost gained back her strength. Mona came up the stairs and embraced Molly, seeing Tom's face and thinking something had gone wrong. She thought they had argued, but couldn't imagine about what.

Both children hugged Molly as she stooped down to put her arms around them. Her legs trembled under her own weight, and dress. "Be easy," she said.

"We *are* easy," both children chimed, and their strength surged into Molly so that when she stood up again her legs did not shake at all.

Later, Tom asked, "Why don't you tell Dad?"

"He'd just worry," and Molly shook her head so that Tom wondered who would lead him when the time came, to a pasture that offered new life. The children played outside.

"Are you going to die?" Tom asked his mother a few days after Christmas, the day before he left.

Molly laughed at him, "Eventually, I hope." Then she said, "No, no Tom. Not soon."

Tom grew irritated with her for some reason (maybe for the possibility of her death or of his own). "You should tell him," he said.

That was a year ago. That was last Christmas.

Annie and Albert took Jacob to the station. They didn't speak of anything except when Jacob might come back for a visit. Then Annie asked if his hand was all right and Jacob said Yes, he thought so. And she said, "Are *you* all right?" which is what she meant when she asked about his hand.

Jacob told them how as a young man he had wanted to leave this town, feeling that the lives here were narrow and unlived. So he left, seeing that the pleasure he sought was not in this place. But he found after years of searching that it was not in any other place either, so he came back and people smiled as if they knew what had been learned, as if they had gone away themselves years ago for the same reason. Then Jacob turned to her, his expression, his face a dry cloth. And there came sudden stretchings around his mouth and eyes and he pressed his hands together.

Annie told him that the look he had was the look he had once when he saw a buffalo for the first time. They were in Yellowstone Park and Jacob got out of the car to see more closely the buffalo whose eyes were a golden-yellow, as though there was fire in that head and those eyes were the holes to see the bright hotness.

"We yelled for you to come back," said Annie (she was telling this to Albert too), "because no one wanted to get out with you, even though there was a slope and the buffalo was twenty feet down the slope."

Jacob remembered and liked hearing Annie tell this now. Annie had for him the magical quality that memory often supplies. He remembered leaning toward the buffalo wanting to see into the hairy frame. And that buffalo saw him too, but wasn't impressed, fairly unimpressed it seemed, even peeved. For, as Annie told him, every buffalo seems cross about something.

"And when we finally called you back in," said Annie, "you talked about his eyes. And I had seen them too. Those eyes stayed with me, but I could tell they stayed even more with you, and helped you to understand something about Time a

216

little better; but it's hard to say how. And that buffalo knew about Time, but he wasn't telling anybody."

They told each other good-bye, Jacob leaning to kiss both Annie and Albert.

Supposedly, Drue was behind him now. That hissing sound that changed at times into the screech of a bad flute, it was gone. But the song he heard now took on the rhythm of a broken-down wagon in which people ride: they watch the movement of the wheels rolling and jerking along and the motion seems almost jolly, but an eminent fear of collapse holds the rider's attention.

The train was well out of town when Jacob heard a young boy's voice from the next car and saw Harley push through the curtain. "Ever catch a fish?" he asked, then smiled, "Hey," he said when he saw Jacob.

"Hey," Jacob was glad to see him. "You still riding this train?"

"My Mama brings me every two weeks to see my dad. It's the law." He scraped his shoe on the floor as though he had stepped in something. "She don't like to though."

"Well," said Jacob and he sat forward to scrape his own shoe, give the boy company. "I'll bet your dad likes to see you."

"He does."

"And you'll get good at riding these trains."

"I already am. I can go two cars, swinging, without putting my feet down but six times."

"That's amazing."

"And I can go to the dining car by myself and order a hot dog or Coke, and they bring it to me. Then either I print my name, or if I have money, I pay."

"That's really something."

"I know." Harley looked up from his shoes. "Want to go there now?"

Jacob said he did.

They ordered hot dogs, plain, hashbrowns and one Coke. Jacob ordered coffee. The waiter poured water for them and called them both Sir. Harley nodded in the way his mother probably would, as an acknowledgment of services.

While they waited, Jacob pointed to a house set back in the woods. It was similar to Annie's. "That's like the house I've been staying in."

"You were there all that time?" the boy asked. It had been almost two months. "You never went home?"

"I thought that *was* home," said Jacob, realizing something. But Harley didn't hear, because for the first time he noticed Jacob's hand. He didn't want to be rude by mentioning it and wondered if Jacob knew, as though it had happened only in the last few moments and maybe Jacob didn't know, maybe he shouldn't tell him. Harley was so intrigued that he didn't hear Jacob and said again, "You never went home? All this time?"

Jacob shook his head.

He would arrive in Virginia just as it became dark—the light going from a deep white to a shiny metallic gray that gave the air the quality of water, not reflecting, but inhabiting the sky. Upon approaching his house, he would see through the window —Molly seated, the cat beside her. There would be a Christmas tree in the corner, already decorated so that the lights reflected in the window.

Jacob would stop outside the window a moment before going in, to look at Molly reading a book. A lamp on the table beside her would throw shadows against the wall that were improbable, immense. When Molly closed the book, Jacob looked to see if she had finished the last page. She hadn't. She closed it slowly, not lifting her hand from it, but looking at it still, the way people used to read from the Bible in a rural church. They would end and close and wait for a moment before speaking, thinking their life might change. And in those moments there

218

was a reverence or a hope, and that is how she looked then when she closed the book. And it was not the Bible she held, and the only thing reverent was what she had read and the fact that when she closed the book, she believed it, believed it might keep her from old age or loss or death. So she kept her hand there, not wanting that moment of when she believed in something to end or to be gone.

"I don't know where I live either," Harley told Jacob. Then Harley said, "Your fingers are gone," and he looked to Jacob as though Jacob might be surprised, maybe even gasp and look to the floor where they had dropped.

"Not all of them," Jacob said and held up both hands.

"Three are gone," Harley told him. "What happened?"

Jacob didn't want to tell the whole story, so he said, "I went deer hunting. Shot a deer."

"That deer bit 'em off?"

"Yeah."

"Ga. You kill him?"

"Yeah."

"Ga. I would have too, if he'd done that to me."

Harley wanted to see the hand close up, so Jacob opened and closed it and held it up for Harley to touch.

"Does it hurt?" Harley wanted to touch the end of the stub, but asked first.

"Not anymore."

The waiter brought hot dogs. Jacob sipped his coffee and ate the hashbrowns, then offered his hot dog to Harley, saying he'd gotten full on the hashbrowns. Harley took it.

Jacob looked out and noticed how all the leaves were off the trees. He hadn't noticed it before now. He spent Thanksgiving recuperating and after that he just hadn't looked, so that now it surprised him, but the surprise was not a good one. He felt as he did sometimes at night when it gets late before he realizes and he feels he has missed something.

219

*   *   *

"Here's Georgia." Jacob's father lit a cigar.

And Jacob pointed to a clearing. "I've seen that place before."

"You been there?" His father didn't know what he meant, but looked anyway.

"No. Well, maybe. I mean it's familiar to me."

His father knew what he meant. "You want to go closer? See it?"

Jacob turned to see the ground recede into the distance. "No sir."

Jacob watched the landscape, forgetting for a moment about Harley. He searched for trees, for the same thing he searched for as a boy on trips. Clearings. He thought as he rode how each season gave itself completely to the next one. How winter light pulls steadily at what is not seen, and in summer the leaves push up to end every trace of spring. How the fall, this fall, had lost everything to cope with winter.

That was what he thought before Harley began to jerk at his sleeve. Jacob turned, startled to see the boy pointing, or rather gesturing with a sort of urgent despair, to a group of trees gathered in a half-circle.

"Look." And Harley kept pulling as if Jacob didn't see it, or as if Harley saw something else, something he recognized or thought he knew. When he spoke, his voice was sheer as wing. "Whose land is that?"

Jacob saw nothing for himself, but he looked for something, a light, a familiar ground. They had already passed it. Harley tugged again. Then Harley stood to let whatever it was draw him to it. He pressed his face against the window. "Whose is that?" he asked again.

And Jacob said, "It's yours now."

*Elizabeth Cox grew up in Chattanooga, Tennessee,
and attended the University of Tennessee in Knoxville
and Chattanooga. She completed her A.B. degree in
English and psychology, at the University of
Mississippi in 1964 and her M.F.A. degree at the
University of North Carolina, Greensboro, in 1979.
Since then Ms. Cox has taught creative writing courses
at Duke University's Continuing Education Program
and has had fellowships at both MacDowell and
Yaddo writers' colonies. Her work has appeared in*
Fiction International *and* Antaeus, *and her story,
"The Land of Goshen," was cited for excellence by*
Pushcart Press *and* Best American Short Stories.
*She lives now in Durham, North Carolina with her
children.* Familiar Ground *is her first novel.*